ELFGIFT

The water spilled on the dying king's forehead.

For a moment, the king's breathing stopped. Then his eyes opened, very blue in the faint light, and staring blindly. He drew another thick, tearing breath, and made some sound.

Everyone was silent, keeping still so that their clothes shouldn't rustle, holding their breath, so that the half-choked, weak voice should be heard.

"King after me," he said. "Elfgift. After me. King. Elfgift."

Also by Susan Price in Point:

ELFGIFT

SUSAN PRICE

Scholastic Children's Books
Commonwealth House, 1–19 New Oxford Street,
London, WC1A 1NU, UK
A division of Scholastic Ltd
London ~ New York ~ Toronto ~ Sydney ~ Auckland
Mexico City ~ New Delhi ~ Hong Kong

First published in the UK by Scholastic Ltd, 1995
This edition, 2000

ISBN 0 439 01397 6

Typeset by TW Typesetting, Midsomer Norton, Somerset
Printed by Cox & Wyman Ltd, Reading, Berks

10 9 8 7 6 5 4 3 2 1

CONTENTS

CHAPTER 1

Death of a King

The candlelight hung in the air of the royal chamber like golden gauze, while deep shadows gathered in the corners, quivering as the light quivered. The air of the room was thick with the smoke of candles and fire, but other scents and stinks came to the nose with the shifting of little draughts and breezes: a sudden sweet or sharp scent from the floor-herbs trodden underfoot, and the stale, bad stinks of long sickness and sweat.

In the centre of the room, in the brightest of the light from the lamps and candles, was a wide bed, its posts carved with dragons and twisting, biting animals. In the bed, propped on many pillows, covered by a blanket sewn with glittering golden

1

threads, lay the dying king. His breathing was heavy and slow, as if a great weight lay on his chest, and every lift of his ribs strained against it.

Around the bed were gathered the Royal Kin, the leading members of the Twelve Hundred. Their shadows were thrown, stretched and mis-shapen, over the walls and ceiling.

To one side of the bed, alone, stood Athelric, the king's only surviving brother. The strong shadows made the jowls and wrinkles of his face seem heavier than they were. By daylight, though ageing, he was still a handsome man, his fair hair and beard having faded rather than greyed. When a man reaches forty, says the poet, the sound of a coffin-nail driven home makes his face change. Athelric was over forty, but when the aeldermen of the council met to choose the next king from among the Royal Kin, they would choose Athelric. That was all but certain. He was still a strong, active man; and he was proven in battle and counsel. Even the fact that he had survived to his present age as the brother of the king spoke in favour of his political skills. Kings grew nervous and jealous, and less talented brothers than Athelric tended to die young. His likeness to the dying king, which was strong, would also count for him with the more sentimental members of the Council – as would the fact that, once his brother was dead, he would be the only pagan remaining among the Royal Kin. There weren't many Christ-followers among the aeldermen.

On the other side of the bed the Christ-followers were gathered – the athelings, their mother the queen, and the foreigner, the Christ-priest, Father Fillan.

Queen Ealdfrith sat in her gilded chair with as much dignity as could be expected from a lady so long dead. In the candlelight, her robes glimmered with gold thread, and jewels shone on her blackened finger-bones. Her still plentiful hair had been gathered under a linen head-dress, held in place by a jewelled circlet. Beneath the white linen, her face had blackened and withered and she bared her teeth at her husband and sons. From her drifted a strong smell which Father Fillan called the odour of sanctity but which, to a less devout or pagan nose, stank like corruption.

When alive, Queen Ealdfrith had been a lady famous for her goodness and learning. Hearing about the faith of Christ, she had sent into the kingdoms of the Northern foreigners, asking that a priest might come and teach her more of it. Father Fillan had come to her, and his preaching had filled her with an enthusiasm for Christ. Some – Athelric was one – suspected that her enthusiasm had more to do with Father Fillan's shaven face and dark eyes than his sermons; but such remarks were to be expected from pagans and men. However it had come about, Ealdfrith abandoned the True Gods, and her life became one of penance for ever having worshipped Them, and more penance for the sins of her unconverted countrymen. From the day Fillan baptized her she never ate more than one meal a day, and that nothing more than bread and water. Summer and winter, she wore only one shift, of rough wool, and her rooms were never warmed by a fire, or lighted by a candle after dark. She was a saint, Father Fillan said; only a saint could have the strength to be so devout, so faithful. But perhaps her very piety made others disinclined to follow her example. Cold, hunger and darkness might be novelties to the Royal Kin, but to most of the queen's subjects they were things too common to have any attraction; and the number of Christ-followers in the land remained small. The queen even failed to convert her own husband. King Eadmund gave her permission to build a small chapel and to worship there if she chose, but he remained true to his ancestor, Woden, and to Thunor, and Ing, and Freyja. So when Queen Ealdfrith died, Father Fillan lost more than a friend. He lost his patron, and the leading member of his congregation and – if certain rumours were correct – a lover.

So he had kept her by him. It had been, he insisted, the queen's own dying wish. King

Eadmund, who had hardly spoken to his wife for many years, had been puzzled by Father Fillan's request, but then, he had found Father Fillan puzzling in many ways – the shaven face, the shaven head, the crawling and grovelling before his single god. Fillan was a foreigner, after all, with foreign ways. And so Queen Ealdfrith, her skin-and-bone body half-mummified and dressed in riches, had become the kingdom's first and only Christian saint; and a fine saint too. More impressive than any to be found in Fillan's own Christ-following North Country. More impressive, even, than many relics owned by cathedrals on the continent. Fillan was proud of his queenly saint, and brought her out on every occasion.

Her youngest son, the atheling Wulfweard, could not keep himself from looking at her. He would give his attention, as was proper, to his dying father but then, with a sudden start, would look again at the saint, as if he suspected her of being about to rise from her chair and embrace him. He had never been easy in his mother's presence. Unwin, the eldest of the athelings, slung an arm around the boy's shoulders, squeezing his arm reassuringly with a big, weapon-calloused hand.

The athelings all had the good looks of their father and uncle, but Unwin, a man of eight and twenty, though tall and strong in body, had inherited the family face at its harshest. The candlelight lit the bosses of his cheekbones, and highlighted the swell of his lips as they pouted to close over his big horse's teeth, while his heavy brows cast his eyes into deep shadow. Where the light touched his hair, it shone a dark, coppery red. He wore it dragged back from his face and bound into a long horse-tail down his back. It was in his nature to wear it so, tied back out of his way, but it did nothing to soften his hard features.

Wulfweard, though as tall as his brother, was no more than six and ten, and beside Unwin seemed slight and flexible as a grass-blade. His hair was worn loose, in the fashion, hanging almost to his waist. His uneasy movements stirred it, and it caught the light with gleams of gold and russet. A harder light sparked from the brooch at his shoulder, the collar about his neck, and the buckle on his belt.

Hunting, the third atheling, stood behind his brothers, further from the light. He stood quietly, his arms folded, his gaze never shifting from the bed.

As the king drew another dragging breath, Unwin looked towards the foot of the bed, towards Father Fillan. He beckoned with a motion of his head, and the priest came forward, withdrawing his hands from his sleeves. He held a small flask.

Athelric saw it and demanded, "What's that?"

No one answered him. The priest came to the head of the bed, and stooped over the king. He was muttering something, and unstoppering the flask. Athelric reached out and took the priest's wrist. "What are you doing?"

"Nothing, Uncle," Unwin said, but Athelric, scowling, wrenched at the priest's arm, pulling him away from the king.

Father Fillan, a much smaller and lighter man than Athelric, said, "I am going to baptize the lord king."

"That you are not!" Athelric said.

"That he might be saved and enter the Kingdom of Heaven," Fillan said. He looked into Athelric's angry face, and refused to let his own face show the pain that the big man was causing him as he bent back his arm.

Unwin took his arm from around Wulfweard and, stepping forward, leaned over the bed to take his uncle's hand from the priest's.

"It is our wish," he said, with a slight movement of his head to indicate his brothers, "that our father be baptized into our faith."

"Spit on your wishes!" Athelric said. "It wasn't *his* wish!"

Unwin looked away from his uncle. To the priest he said, "Finish the baptism."

Father Fillan, withdrawing out of Athelric's

reach, pulled the stopper from the flask of holy water, and once more approached the bed.

"You do wrong!" Athelric said. Unwin said nothing, but nodded to the priest. Wulfweard again drew close to his eldest brother, while looking from the corner of his eyes at the stick-like corpse of his mother, sitting in its chair.

The priest stooped over the bed, muttering his foreign words, the bottle poised to pour the holy water.

Athelric raised his clenched fist over the bed, in the sign of Thunor's Hammer. The light of a lamp threw the shadow of the fist, the Hammer, gigantically over the ceiling and the whole room.

The water spilled on the dying king's forehead.

For a moment the king's breathing stopped. Then his eyes opened, very blue in the faint light, and staring blindly. He drew another thick, tearing breath, and made some sound.

Father Fillan straightened and drew back in some astonishment. Had the holy water made a cure? The others in the room moved sharply towards the bed, all of them, stooping over it.

Athelric, leaning over the king, said, "Eadmund?"

The king's vague eyes moved to him, and perhaps saw him. Perhaps he only recognized the voice, but he said, "Athelric – "

Unwin, leaning from the other side, and trying to push his uncle aside, said, "Father!"

Athelric pushed him away, saying, "Ssh! Ssh!" The king was speaking.

Everyone was silent, keeping still so that their clothes wouldn't rustle, holding their breath, so that the half-choked, weak voice should be heard.

"King after me," he said. "Elfgift. After me. King. Elfgift." His hand, fumbling from under the covers, found Athelric's and clasped his brother's weakly. He stared into the candle-smeared gloom above him, perhaps seeing his brother's face, perhaps seeing nothing, but he repeated, once more, "Elfgift!" And then the lids drooped, and the strength left the hand which Athelric held, and there was only the rough, painful breathing to show that a little life still remained.

Unwin straightened and stared across the bed at his uncle, who stood as astonished. Then Unwin laughed and said, "Elfgift, Uncle. He's named the bastard as his successor."

Athelric said, "It's for the Council to choose."

"But the king's choice counts for something. Perhaps you won't be our king, after all."

"One good thing," Athelric said. "The king won't be a Christ-follower!"

"It would be a terrible thing," Father Fillan said, "a great sin, for that – creature – to become king."

Athelric swung towards him. "What do you know? The first king of our line was elf-born – the son of Woden!"

"Do you want the *next* king to be?" Unwin asked, and laughed again when Athelric's face turned baffled.

King Eadmund had taken many concubines, and had fathered many bastards – exactly how many was not known. If their mothers had been married and of the Twelve Hundred, the nobles, then the children went by the name of their mother's husband, even when it was well known who their true father was. If the mother was noble, but unmarried, then it had never been too hard to find a husband for her before the child was born. And peasant women and peasant bastards could be forgotten, though a small grant of land might be given to an especial favourite, perhaps even with a gift of freedom. There were plenty of bastards among the peasants, and no objections to another child who could be put to work.

Queen Ealdfrith had never minded her husband's mistresses. Theirs had been a political marriage, and she had not expected love or fidelity from her husband. Besides, once Father Fillan had brought Christ to her court, she had followed her own interests: praying and starving. But that *thing*; that thing hadn't even been a woman.

It had been one of those things sent into the world by the Devil, a demon whose whole desire was to prick men on to lying, and thieving, to murder and greed, lust, envy and all the other sins that made life on Earth such misery. It had emerged from the forest, that wild, unblessed place, in the shape of a woman – the shape only – and because it wasn't its true shape, it had been able to take on an appearance of unearthly beauty. It had put the king under a spell. When the stories had come to the queen's court – the predictably romantic stories – of the king finding the beauty in the forest while he was hunting, and carrying her home before him on his horse, the queen had shrieked aloud in outrage. It had been an insult not only to her, but to her new faith. The Devil, threatened by the coming of Christ, was trying to destroy the new faith while it was still weak.

"She was so beautiful, the elf-woman," Athelric said, looking down at his brother's face. "So beautiful – she was ugly, she was so beautiful. You looked at her and the skin crept down your back."

"Did you ever see her back?" Unwin asked, and Hunting laughed. The wood-spirits, it was said – call them elves or devils – could never completely disguise themselves as human, and would never turn their backs to you because, however beautiful they seemed, from behind they looked like riven, rotten, hollowed-out trees.

"What would you know?" Athelric said. "You never saw her. You were at prayer with your mother." With a sneer and a sweep of his hand, he indicated Father Fillan and the bejewelled corpse.

Unwin's big, thick-lipped mouth pouted more as he closed it tightly against making any answer. He understood the taunt – to Athelric's thinking any man who prayed to a Prince of Peace who had advised his followers to invite another blow when someone struck them, was a coward and a weakling.

Father Fillan said firmly, "The creature was a devil. The proof is that it died on the birth of the king's son. It could not withstand the spark of God's creation in even a half-mortal child."

Athelric was about to ask if every woman who died giving birth was therefore a devil, when the king began to choke, and once more drew the attention of everyone. "I must give him the last rites," Father Fillan said.

Athelric held out a long arm, the hand pointing, fending the priest off. "You will keep away! Come near, speak one word of your filthy spells, and I'll knock you flat!" And bending low over the king, Athelric kissed his forehead. "Go well. Make your way safely to Woden's Hall."

Quietly, Father Fillan began to speak a prayer for the dead. The king's choking breaths stopped, while the prayer went whispering on. Otherwise, there was silence, except for one gasp from Wulfweard. Unwin pressed the boy to his chest. The light of the candles glimmered over the corpse, which was so fragile that its presence barely lifted the covers from the mattress.

The prayer mumbled to an end, and there was a deep silence in the room. Unwin cleared his throat before speaking. "The Council can never choose the bastard," he said. He coughed again. "There is no need to mention that our father ever—"

"I shall put the name before them myself," Athelric said. He and Unwin considered each other across the bed. In answer to Unwin's unspoken question, Athelric said, "My brother and king named him his successor. It's my duty to put his name before the Council, and I shall do so." He came to the foot of the bed and paused, looking at the priest. "My brother will be buried *properly*. In a ship, with a king's goods." Athelric left the room.

Silence settled over the room again. Wulfweard was leaning his head on Unwin's shoulder, encircled by his brother's arm. Hunting, slightly taller than Unwin, came to stand shoulder to shoulder with him. Hunting said, "The half-thing might not even be alive any more."

Father Fillan said, "My lords, I think it is." Hunting and Unwin looked at him. The priest, like so many Christ-priests, could read and write, and often knew surprising things. "When it was born, and the devil died, your father had the thing placed with a wet-nurse – a woman of no standing. But he made a grant of land to support the thing.

13

I saw the charter. The land was in Hornsdale."

"That doesn't mean it's still alive," Hunting said.

"No, my lord, but a while ago – a year, perhaps a little longer – I heard talk of a healer in Hornsdale. And this healer was said to be – well, uncanny. Not altogether human. Which made me wonder."

"The Devil has turned healer?" Unwin said.

"The Devil will often seem to do good, in order to fool us and lead us into sin. Its touch may take away the body's pain, but it damns and destroys the soul."

"Hornsdale," Unwin repeated, and the priest nodded.

The door opened, and in came attendants, women carrying cloths and bowls of water, to wash the king's body and prepare him for his lying in state. Father Fillan saw Unwin glance at Hunting and signal to him, with his eyes, to follow. Guiding Wulfweard with him, Unwin left the room, and Hunting went after.

Fillan took up his place behind the chair of his dead and sainted queen, and began to recite prayers for the dead king. He had baptized the man, and considered his soul to be in his care. And, if he could manage it, the king would have a Christian burial.

*   *   *

Unwin had his own lodgings within the complex of buildings that made up the Royal Residence, but he didn't lead his brothers there, nor to their lodgings. He took them to that part of the Residence where the royal pigsties and the royal hen-houses and sheep-pens were to be found. Even there he kept well clear of the buildings, where pig-herds or hen-wives might be lying wakeful. Privacy was hard to come by in a Royal Residence. Even in your private lodgings, where you thought yourself quite alone, you could never tell who stood outside, at the low thatched eaves of the house, and eavesdropped.

Putting his arms over the shoulders of his brothers, Unwin drew them both close to him, so that he could whisper and still be heard. "Hunting, I want you to get together a company of men; ten should be more than enough. At first light I want you to go to—"

"Hornsdale," Hunting said.

Unwin's face could hardly be seen in the darkness, but his head nodded.

Wulfweard asked, "Why?" With their father's funeral so close, he was thinking, Hunting shouldn't be riding off on errands.

Both his brothers laughed. Hunting leaned over, kissed his cheek and said, "That's why he hasn't asked you to go."

Unwin shook out his cloak and threw half of it

around Wulfweard. They stood close together, huddled in the warmth of the one cloak against the damp chill of the night.

"Think!" Unwin ordered.

"This Elfgift isn't a danger to you," Wulfweard said. "He's just a bastard – he's not even of the Twelve Hundred. He can't be chosen king."

"But our father named him successor," Unwin said. "And Athelric is going to speak for him to the Council."

"But that doesn't matter. The Council choose, and the Council –" Wulfweard fell silent as he felt Unwin's arm tighten around him.

"Why," Unwin asked, "why is Athelric speaking for this bastard elf's drop? Athelric wants to be king. So why is he going to put the bastard's name before the Council?"

Unwin, with tilted head, looked into Wulfweard's face as he waited for an answer. Hunting stood by with folded arms.

"I don't know," the boy said.

Unwin shook him gently. "Think it through. Athelric's son is dead. He has only daughters. He's an old man. He can't hope to rule for long. After him, who will the Council choose?"

"You," Wulfweard whispered.

"And I am for Christ. I'll tell you what Athelric means to do. He means to tell the Council that our father named Elfgift his successor, and he will have the thing brought into the Twelve Hundred. They will still make him king, he knows. He will marry one of his daughters to the thing. Then, by the time he dies, he will have worked on them so that they choose the bastard as king after him – a *pagan* king. A pagan line." From a distance, from the walls of the Residence, came the cough of a guard, loud and sudden in the dark.

"And long before Athelric's death," Hunting said, "we would all be in our graves."

"You would break your neck out hunting, Hunting," Unwin said.

"You would eat something bad and puke yourself to death."

"And our little Wulf," said Unwin, hugging his youngest brother, "would maybe be bitten by a mad dog."

"A shame, but not a Christian atheling left," said Hunting.

"No one to choose but Elfgift."

Wulfweard said, in astonishment, "Uncle Athelric wouldn't do that!"

Hunting gave a short laugh, and said, "Stupid!"

"No," said Unwin, who knew the difference between stupidity and innocence. He hugged Wulfweard hard to him, and looked at Hunting over the boy's head. "Good luck with your hunting in Hornsdale – and our lives will be a little longer."

He saw Hunting nod in the darkness, and watched as his brother's shape quickly dwindled into the night. He kissed Wulfweard's head, and then turned the boy about, walking with him back towards their lodgings. He could trust his brothers as yet, he supposed, while the Council was unlikely to name any of them king. He would be sorry, truly sorry, if Wulfweard ever became a threat... But he would be a fool to suppose that the boy never would.

CHAPTER 2

The Elf-Born

Every day, bread had to be made. Grain was ground into a coarse flour which, mixed with water and a little salt, was made into unleavened bread. It was baked on a hot stone beside the fire, shaped into thin, flat cakes, to cook quicker. There had to be enough to satisfy everyone's hunger, and it was long, boring work. The grain had to be fetched from the storehouse across the yard, a heavy load to be lugged back to the house. It was ground in the quern behind the door. Hild always said they were lucky to have a quern like that: two big grindstones, one on top of the other, with a strong wooden handle to turn the upper one. But then, Hild never used it.

19

Handful by handful the grain from the basket was dropped into the upper stone's central hole. Then the upright wooden handle was grasped in both hands, and the upper stone was turned – dragged, rather – from side to side with a noise of rasping. Stone-dust and flour-dust flew. The grain, crushed and powdered, filtered out from between the stones as flour, and fell on to the smooth leather hide beneath the quern. Kneeling at the quern cramped thè legs, and the effort of turning the heavy stone made the arms and back and shoulders ache. Every now and again there was a pause, a short rest, as the flour from the hide was scooped up into a bowl.

The work was never done. The flour didn't keep as well as the grain, so every day the quern had to be turned again. Every day, the same boring trip to the storehouse, the same heavy basket to be carried across the yard, the same leg-cramping, back-aching, boring turning of the quern-stone. And because it was such a wearying, wearisome chore, it was the job of the least important member of the household, and that meant the bond-girl, Ebba. Turning the quern, day after day after day was what her life was for.

Ebba knew better than to think she could ever get out of the chore. If she had refused to do any of her daily tasks her mistress, Hild, would have been as surprised as if the door-post had spoken –

and then she would have been furious. Ebba was afraid of Hild's temper. So she endured her daily grind, and tried to think of other things while she worked. She concentrated hard on the pictures in her head, trying not to notice what she was doing at all, trying not to hear the monotonous noise of the quern, trying not to feel the ache in her back. Sometimes she told herself stories, or sang over songs under her breath, but most often she thought about Elfgift, because she thought about him all the time anyway. Thoughts of him came into her head even when she had made up her mind not to care about him any more. She loved him. So often had she stared at him that, as she worked the quern, she could quite clearly see him before her open eyes, lit by the fire, the beautiful shape of his face brought out in flame-light and shadow. She could see his thick cap of hair, brown in shadow, but gleaming gold and red, like polished bronze, when he ducked from the house into the light of the yard. Round and round went the heavy quern, while she watched Elfgift walking in her mind, and smiling. Taller than anyone else, he was, and wide across the shoulders, but when he turned sideways, slender as a long-dog. And such a smile!

"Mooning!" Hild would say, if she knew what Ebba was thinking. "Wasting your time mooning over him. Why would he want you, skinny, funny-looking object that you are? Why would any man want you, come to that? No meat on you, no shape. He ain't even going to look at you."

Well, you're wrong, *wrong*, Ebba thought, and ground hard with the quern. Elfgift had done more than look at her, *three times*. Once he had simply caught hold of her hand as they all sat round the fire, had pulled her to her feet and out into the yard, where he'd led her to the little, private house he'd built for himself, where he sometimes ate and slept alone. Not that night, though! The second time he'd called to her and beckoned as she'd been crossing the yard, and she'd gone to him. And the third time he'd sent one of the farm men to tell her to go to the little house. She'd run! Every time she'd thought: now he loves me. Now I'm going to start to be happy. He'll marry me, she thought. I'll be his wife, and not a slave. Everyone would have to treat her differently then.

None of that had happened. He hadn't said he loved her – hadn't said anything much to her at all. He hadn't hurt her or been unkind – but he hadn't been kind either. She had loved him so much, had been so eager to please him that she'd been in pain with it – and he had taken no more and no less notice of her than he always had. Ebba, the girl who ground the flour, and did all the heavy, dirty work that Hild didn't want to do. He smiled at her occasionally, but was as likely to walk straight past her without even seeing her. Weeks, months had gone by before he remembered her the second, the third time. And it was so hard to bear, because she knew exactly how deep her hand could sink into his hair, exactly how thick and soft it was. She knew just how smooth the skin of his back and chest was, and the exact, almost plush, texture of his skin – and yet she could never reach out and touch his hair or touch his skin. She could only long to touch him. Holding back the tears made her throat swell and ache, but she couldn't cry, or Hild would notice. And the quern had to be kept turning.

When she was being sensible, she knew it was impossible that she could have any importance for Elfgift. He was free-born, and owned the farm. Owen, the headman, and the men who worked the fields and looked after the animals, and the farm's other two women – they were all his slaves. Even Hild, who had reared him from a child and called herself his mother, even she was really just one of his slaves, and if she angered him, he could make her feel it. Ebba could remember a couple of times when Hild's face had glowed painfully red because Elfgift had tired of her nagging and had said something bitter to her in front of the others. Once he had asked her if she wanted a whipping, which, as her owner, he had a right to order. It had been a most terrible set-down for Hild, who liked to queen it over the household, and Ebba had secretly been delighted – but even she couldn't help but feel a bit sorry for poor old Hild. It was frightening too – because if Elfgift could treat Hild so badly, what could she expect, the least valuable and important of his possessions?

But she *would* make him love her, she would because she had to, because if she didn't then there was no point in being alive. Life would just be day after day after day of grinding grain. She kept from sobbing, but tears fell on to the quern-stone, and her throat pained her still more. He'd lain with her three times, so he had to like her a little bit. That was a start. She would show him how much she loved him. At meals, she would pass him anything he wanted, even before he could ask for it. When food was short, she would give him hers. She would – she would – do *anything*. And he would see that she really, truly loved him, and so he would love her, and he wouldn't care that she was bony and funny-looking. He would love her. When he saw how much she loved him, he would *have* to love her.

"Love!" Hild said. "You think too much on love – and *he* don't love. He don't love me, and look what I done for him, ever since he was a babby. *They* don't love, his mother's people…"

24

There it was: Elfgift's mother had been an elf-woman out of the forest. From her he had his great beauty, and his gift for healing, and the knack he sometimes showed of knowing what was going to happen before it did. But from her came also his peculiar nature. He would spend a day soothing the sick child of some beggarwoman, who could pay him neither in goods nor favour, and then snub a wealthy landowner who only wanted him to remove a wart – which he could easily do. Then, when some other poor folk came, expecting help since they'd heard how he'd helped others, he would order them to clear off his land before he set his men on them. There was no guessing how he would behave. Neither pity nor hope of gain nor fear of disapproval seemed to guide him.

Sometimes he would feed one of the farm cats titbits, and stroke its head and rub its ears and back until the creature was in ecstasy, rolling on its side and leaning its head on him, purring so loudly it could be heard all through the house. The next time it came near him, he might knock it aside irritably, or simply ignore it. He treated Ebba exactly the same. He was fond of her when he was fond; and she was as silly in response as the fondled cat. But when his mood changed, it changed utterly, and then he had no use for her.

"Or if they do love," Hild said, "it ain't what we mean by love. You be glad he don't love you.

Wouldn't do you any good if he did. There's no luck in loving him."

But Hild was jealous of Elfgift, and didn't want him to love or marry any woman, because then she'd lose her place as headwoman on the farm. But he'll marry *me*, Ebba thought, dragging at the quern so hard she hurt her back. Then I won't be a slave and I'll be above Hild, and I'll give *her* a kick whenever I please. But she knew she would never dare to kick Hild, even if she was Elfgift's wife.

She heard Hild's voice raised outside in the yard, and the note in it caught her attention, so that she raised her head from her work over the quern. Hild's voice sounded angry and urgent. Something was happening, something unusual. Ebba was quick to pick up any hint of anything out of the ordinary happening.

Hild came stumping into the house, ducking under the low doorway.

"Bloody people," she said. "Always coming here, poking about, making a nuisance of themselves. Who wants 'em?"

Ebba lowered her head again and went on querning, asking no questions. If you asked questions, Hild got annoyed with you. If you kept quiet, then she grumbled out everything there was to know sooner or later.

Hild looked round the dimly-lit house. It was dry, warm and comfortable, but it wasn't handsome or even tidy, with straw mattresses and blankets strewn over the sleeping benches, and plates and bowls scattered about in the mess. "Well, it'll have to do," she said. "If folks will come without any say-so, they must take we as they find we." Ebba still said nothing, but the grinding of the quern went on. "Owen won't be pleased," Hild said, "being fetched from his work at this time of day. Don't suppose Gift'll even come. And it's *his* fault." And Hild went out into the yard again.

Ebba knew everything she wanted to know, and went on grinding flour with a more willing spirit and more energy. Soon there'd be a break. Soon Owen would come, and then the visitors, and no one would expect her to go on grinding, not even Hild.

Since the gossip about Elfgift had been going around the countryside, more and more visitors had come to the farm, without any invitation or arrangement. There'd always been a lot of curiosity about Elfgift, because of the stories told about his parents. People found some excuse to walk over and have a look at him. But they were often disappointed because they expected him to have green hair or horse's ears or goat's eyes or horns on his head. Still, they went away and reported that he *was* uncommonly good-looking; and every now and again someone would turn up on some thin excuse, and hang around, obviously waiting to get a look at Elfgift. It wasn't easy because Elfgift didn't like being looked at.

The visitors had grown worse since the story had been spread that Elfgift could heal. At first it was just the poorer folk from the valleys and hills round about. They'd turn up, tired after their trudge, carrying a sick child, or one that had tumbled into a fire and been burnt, or one born with some deformity. Or they'd come carrying some sick man or woman in a blanket, someone with a cut gone bad, or a bashed head from a fall or a fight. What happened then depended on Elfgift. He usually took a look, at least, at the sick person. Sometimes he soothed or healed with great gentleness and kindness, even sweetness. Whatever he did, the visitors took another good story away with them and, as a result, even more people came, from even further away. It didn't seem to matter that some people had been refused healing, or curtly told that they would die in a few days' time. Some even brought sick animals. Elfgift healed them as often as he did people.

"I wish he'd send 'em all away," Hild said. "They'd soon stop coming once that got about. But as long as he keeps helping some of 'em – and I'm fool enough to feed 'em, and we all hodge up and make room for 'em by the fire – well, 'course they'm going to keep coming. Pests."

Those who came from a distance were usually richer than those from nearby. They had to be, to be able to travel. Hild hated them, because they so plainly considered themselves above her, and because they expected everyone on the farm to forget all their work and fawn around them. So Hild said, anyway. Ebba thought some of them pleasant people. And if Elfgift helped them, they usually left some present behind them. "They come here," Hild said, "bringing a pack of folk with 'em. They eat up our stores, they waste our lights, they keep us from our work – and then they give you some useless trinket and act as if they'm giving you the land and the sky! These rich folk ain't as generous as they like to think they be."

So Ebba guessed, from Hild's annoyance, that a party of rich travellers was coming to the farm; and Hild had sent one of the farm-boys running to fetch the men from the fields. Come on, come on, Ebba thought, as she querned more energetically than she had all day. Hurry, hurry. She wanted to see them, the travellers. Perhaps they would have wonderful clothes. Perhaps they would have food with them, which they might share. So entertained was she by the prospect of seeing the travellers that she almost forgot about Elfgift for a few minutes. But not entirely. There would be some poor, sick member of the travellers' party – some little child, she decided. And Elfgift would be kind this time; he would cure the child, and its parents would be so grateful. She would be proud of Elfgift. It was always pleasant to see other people admire him. And when everyone was in such a good mood, Elfgift would turn to her and say, "And I'm going to marry Ebba…"

She paused a little in her grinding as she heard another voice in the yard. It was Owen. He was complaining about being fetched from his work: the fields were being ploughed and sown and manured.

"Is he coming?" Hild asked. "They'm almost here."

Owen laughed, and Ebba guessed from the tone of the laugh that Elfgift wasn't coming to greet their guests. And a few moments later brought all the din of arrival: thumping of horses' hooves, jangling of harness, creaking of wagons, shouting of men – a huge, exciting noise. These must indeed be rich people. Ebba jumped up, brushing flour from her plain, limp grey dress, and hurried out into the yard. No one noticed her. She was small and of no importance and their attention was all elsewhere.

It was on the horses carrying armed men which were treading among the honking, scattering geese in the muddy yard. Each man wore a leather shirt sewn with metal rings, and a leather cap. One of the men carried a spear, another had a quiver of arrows and a bow slung at his back. A big wagon had pulled up outside the farm's thorn hedge, and more armed men rode on the wagon. This truly was a rich party, possibly the richest that had ever come. Ebba hugged herself. There would be things to see!

Another horse came through the farm-gate, and a man swung himself down. A cloak of smooth, fine blue cloth swung from his shoulders, over a tunic of green and blue check. Gold glittered at his wrists and on his fingers. What wealth there was in the cloth he wore alone! Weeks and weeks of women's work, of spinning and weaving. The man was looking around at the farm-buildings, the store-sheds, the little houses for the poultry, the cattle-sheds and pigsties, and the little house itself. He plainly didn't think much of it nor, when he looked at Hild and Owen, did he think much of them. Ebba was pleased to see him despise Hild, but annoyed too. After all, the whole farm, and Hild and everything, belonged to Elfgift and no one, she thought, should despise anything of Elfgift's.

"This is the home of the healer?" the rich stranger asked. "The elf-born?"

Both Hild and Owen assured him that it was, and were explaining that Elfgift wasn't at home just at the moment, when the stranger cut them short.

"I shall be staying for a while, until the healer's helped my wife. I am Morcar Sweynssen – I'm a trader out of the Danelaw – " As he said this, he turned away to watch a small woman being helped down from the wagon by one of the armed men. Her hair was covered by a neat, white linen head-dress, and her body was swathed in a cloak of bright red. Ebba crept a little further from the house to get a better look. The cloak had slits for the woman's arms and, as she was led towards her husband, it could be seen that it fastened down the front with little silver buttons. Ebba's envy was as great as her admiration. She wanted a beautiful, warm cloak like that so much that it hurt – but she knew that she would never, never have one.

"My wife is Aldgytha," Morcar said, taking her hand. He looked around again. "I hope there is somewhere we can stay?"

Owen took a small step backwards and shrank into himself, making it clear that he had nothing to say. This left it up to Hild, and even she was tongue-tied by the wealth of these people. Shyly she waved a hand towards the house, moving towards it at the same time. "Please," she said, "come inside." Aldgytha raised her cloak and skirts to clear the dirt, and took little steps, trying to avoid the worst of the mud and muck. Morcar put his arm around her, as if to help.

Ebba, panicking, ducked into the house before them, and scuttled over the blankets and palliasses, right to the further end. So she saw them come in, ducking lower than was necessary, and then straightening to look about them with faces in which politeness and dismay were equally mixed.

Ebba looked about too. None of the farm-buildings were much more than head-height and all of them had low doorways, because it was easier to build them that way. But everyone was used to it, and it wasn't until Ebba saw this rich couple duck so low and seem so surprised as they straightened that it occurred to her that it might be more convenient to have higher buildings and higher doorways.

One room had always seemed enough, too, until she saw Morcar and Aldgytha stare about them with such carefully polite faces. And then she noticed the rough plasterwork of the low walls, and the way that the soot and smoke from years and years of fires had blackened the walls, and the thin rafters and the thatch, until it smutched anything which touched it. Aldgytha's beautiful linen head-dress and scarlet cloak were going to get dirtied just by her sitting down in their house! No wonder she seemed dismayed.

The guests were standing in the central passage which ran from one side of the house to the other. In front of them was the room where everyone lived and slept and ate. Behind them, on the other side of the passage, was a byre where animals could be housed at night. A rich, round reek drifted from it, of animal dung and sweat. Morcar looked over his shoulder at the byre. Then he said, to Hild: "Have you nowhere better than this?"

It was exactly what Hild hated about these people. And Ebba, though she would normally have been pleased to see Hild embarrassed, was angry too, because this was Elfgift's house they were criticizing.

"Sorry, master," Hild said. "This is our house. This is where we live."

Morcar nodded. Then he guided his wife over the tumbled covers and palliasses and saw her seated in a warm place by the central fire. "Are you hungry?" he asked her. "Thirsty?" She made some reply. "Wait a little while," he said. "I'll see things unpacked."

And, ignoring Hild, and never noticing Ebba, Morcar went out into the yard and started yelling at his men. Things were unpacked from the wagon and brought into the house. Furs, cushions, cups, plates, leather jugs of drink and little packages of food. Aldgytha was made comfortable with cushions packed around her, and was served a little meal by one of Morcar's men. Ebba tried to see what Aldgytha was eating from her place at the back of the house, but couldn't, and was afraid to leave her place in case Morcar would be angry.

Morcar turned to Hild, who was still standing in the central passage, too furious to move, and said to her, in a friendly fashion, "I could see there was plenty of room in the sheds."

Hild looked at him. "In the sheds, master?"

"For your people," he said. He gestured towards his wife at the fire. "We'll take this place. Your people can sleep in the sheds for a night or two. Just until we've seen the healer."

Hild couldn't close her mouth. She stared and said nothing.

"Now, where is the healer?" Morcar asked.

"Working, master," Hild managed.

"Working?" he said, as if that was a surprise to him.

"In the fields, master," Hild said. "There's ploughing, this time of year. And sowing and mucking. A lot to be done, master." And you're keeping us from it, her tone implied.

"Of course," he said. "Well, the sooner we see him, the better." He looked at her, and seemed to be waiting for something. "Well?" he said, again.

"What, master?" Hild asked.

"Well, send for the healer. Fetch him here."

With some satisfaction, Hild said, "Oh, he knows you're here, master. We already told him. He won't come."

Morcar was taken aback. "Won't come?"

Then, perhaps remembering that this healer was free-born, he said, "Show me where he is and I'll go and talk to him."

Hild went out into the yard and Morcar followed. Ebba, knowing Hild so well, could tell from the way she moved that she was delighted to give the man directions on how to find Elfgift. She knew what kind of greeting he was likely to get when he started demanding that Elfgift leave what he was doing and return to the house, and then give up his house to the visitors and sleep in the sheds.

Still outside, Hild began calling Ebba's name. In a fright, forgetting shyness, Ebba scrambled from her place and back to the quern. Aldgytha looked up, startled, from her meal of small beer and white bread, as the girl appeared, from nowhere, and began turning the noisy quern.

Hild, ducking back into the house, said, "Oh, there you are. When's that flour going to be done? It is all right, isn't it, my lady, if the girl goes on querning there? Only we got to make bread. And the quern's a heavy thing to carry out to the sheds."

"Oh, yes! Yes!" Aldgytha said meekly.

Ebba kept her head down and kept grinding, while Hild began bad-temperedly to prepare a mess of boiled oats and vegetables in the iron pot. Hild was proud of that pot but Ebba, peeping

36

from her work, saw Aldgytha giving a shocked look at the old, caked food around its edge. Aldgytha hadn't taken off her red cloak. Ebba looked at the strips of embroidery that hemmed the arm-slits, and at the little silver buttons. She also noticed the way Aldgytha sat, drawn into herself, as if she wished to touch as little of her surroundings as possible.

Morcar came back while Ebba was mixing with water the flour she had finally finished grinding, to make the bread. Ignoring the girl, he sat beside his wife, and accepted from her a slice of the white bread they had brought with them. It wasn't really white, but it was the palest brown Ebba had ever seen. "He is coming," he said to his wife. "I talked to him, and he is coming."

Yes, Ebba thought, he would come with the other men, at the end of the day, to eat, as he always did; not before. She was looking forward to his return even more than usual.

The men came home late in the afternoon, when it was already growing dusk. They came ducking into the house, hunched, dark shapes dimly seen by the light of the fire. They were dressed in tunics of grey, undyed, homespun wool, worn for so many years that they were shapeless and limp. They brought a smell with them, which rapidly filled the whole house: a thick, salty smell of old sweat soaked into their clothes and staled; a smell of the earth, and of manure. Aldgytha covered her little nose with her little hand.

"What?" Morcar said. "Why have you come in here? Haven't you been told?"

The men stayed at the door, peering shyly at the newcomers. Elfgift came in behind them. He was taller than any of them, and could only stand upright directly under the point of the roof. The last light from the open doorway caught his hair and made it shine red. He pushed through the knot of his farm-men, and stooped and snatched up one of Morcar's cushions. Straightening, he hurled it the length of the house. There was a cry as it hit one of the Dane's servants. By then Elfgift had rolled up a fur, which he also threw – and another fur after it, and a cushion after that.

Morcar was silent from surprise. Hild cried, "Elf! The fire!" She was always afraid of things falling into the fire. The whole house would be in flames in a moment and they would all have to sleep in the outhouses.

Elfgift took no notice. More cushions and bundled furs flew through the air. One struck the flimsy roof and fell down, falling on Aldgytha, who squealed. Morcar struggled to his feet, not finding it easy in the cramped house, with the unsteady floor of furs and cushions.

Elfgift faced him, and as Morcar made the first

grunt of speech, Elfgift said, "This be *my* house. My people will sleep in here, where they always sleep, in their own places. But I'm generous. I'll let you share it." And then Elfgift turned his back on Morcar and ducked out of the house again.

Morcar started to follow, but Owen stepped in his way. "I'd leave him, master." Morcar made as if to pass him, but Owen said, "Healers can blast as well as heal, master." Then Morcar thought better of it and returned to his wife. He ordered his servants to move their gear to the back of the house, making room for the farm-people close to the door. Sitting beside Aldgytha, he put his arms round her and told her not to be frightened. Ebba, sent to offer them some of the farm's bread, heard him tell his wife, "Remember, the man's only a churl. He doesn't know how to behave. But I'll get around him, you'll see."

Ebba went back to Hild and said, "I'll take Elfgift's food to him."

Hild gave her a squinting look. "I'll bet you will," she said. But she filled a bowl with the mess from the pot, added a couple of cakes of bread, and gave it to Ebba to carry across the yard.

Behind the main house was Elfgift's small hut. Ebba trudged through the mud, carefully carrying the bowl and the bread. Reaching the hut, she balanced the bowl and bread in the crook of one arm while she knocked on the door; then she lifted the latch and pushed the door open. Inside it was dark and she couldn't see much. There was no fire.

"I've brought you something to eat, master." The little hut had a sleeping bench of hard-packed earth, and she put the bowl and the bread down on the end of it.

She waited for some kind of response and, after a long time, Elfgift's voice said from the darkness, "Thank you, Ebba. That was kind."

Ebba glowed and longed to earn more such praise. "It's cold, master. I could fetch you some fire from the house. Shall I?"

"Go away, Ebba."

"But shall I fetch the fire, master?"

"Ebba. Go away."

Ebba pulled the door shut and went back across the yard to the house, thinking she would take him the fire anyway. He needed it. It would show how much she loved him, even if it made him angry. Once back inside the house, she told Hild that Elfgift wanted a fire.

"Well, why didn't he take it with him, blast him?" Hild said. But she gathered embers and little burning bits from the fire, put them into a bowl, and sent Ebba back across the yard.

Once more Ebba, shivering in the cold wind, knocked at the door of the little hut. "I brought you some fire, master."

There was a noise inside and then the door

opened. Ebba couldn't see Elfgift: it was too dark. She went inside, carrying the bowl of fire, and Elfgift closed the door after her. There was a fire already laid on the hearth of the hut, as there always was, and she knelt and got it going with the live fire from her pot. When the fire was burning and lighting the small interior, she turned to go, but found Elfgift, goldenly lit, leaning against the door.

"Shall I stay then?" she said, and couldn't help simpering. She was to stay, and that was all she wanted in the world. She was happy.

Over in the main house the farm-people, fed, and tired out after a long day, soon fell asleep. Huddled together under their covers, they snored comfortably through the night. For Morcar, Aldgytha and their company, the night wasn't so good. The squalid little hut was not what they were used to, and its owner seemed of a violent temper. They couldn't help but feel uneasy. Then, too, the fleas of the healer's household seemed livelier than their own, and to appreciate a taste of new blood. Tomorrow, Morcar promised himself, he would make the healer cure his wife, and then they would leave this place. That day the healer had taken him by surprise, but he would be ready tomorrow and, ready, he knew how to deal with a fellow like that.

Morcar and Aldgytha fell asleep in the cold early hours of the morning, but had not had nearly enough sleep before they were disturbed by the noise of the household getting up. The open door let in a piercingly cold draught which cleared the fug of the night, and there was a great chorus of coughing and farting and raking of scurfy heads with horny nails. Shouts and whistles and the thumping of hooves accompanied the animals being driven out; and then there was a great deal of unnecessary din in the yard. Inside, meanwhile, Hild unbanked the fire and built it up, groaning loudly as she moved, and giving heavy sighs at frequent intervals. She tramped back and forth between the fire and the yard, and then she started to wallop the iron pot. And the noise of that infernal quern started. Morcar's servants rose then, and began to quarrel with Hild about how and where they should serve breakfast for their master and mistress. Obviously, there was to be no sleep for the master and mistress.

Morcar sat up blearily, and Aldgytha, beside him, peered from beneath her covers and scratched.

"Where is the healer?" Morcar demanded. "He has to see my wife today."

The old woman at the fire squinted at him through the smoke that was adding more layers of soot to the walls and thatch. "You've missed him, master. He's already gone to the fields." The girl kneeling behind the door and turning the quern looked over her shoulder at him in what Morcar felt was an insolent way. What business of hers was their talk?

"But he'll be coming back for his breakfast. I shall speak to him then."

"Please yourself, master," Hild said, continuing with the making of the porridge that, with bread left over from yesterday, would be the breakfast.

Morcar and Aldgytha ate their own breakfast of their pale brown bread, cheese and small beer. And, after a couple of hours of waiting, when the day was brightening into the full morning light, the farm-people came back for their breakfast. The elf-born healer entered last and stood in the door-way, under the point of the roof, while the others had their bowls filled. Each then collected his or her own spoon from a rack on the wall, and scuffled into places on the floor. Once they had eaten, they would lick their spoons clean and put them back in the rack.

With great rudeness, the healer had deliberately turned his back towards his guests. Despite that, Aldgytha noted his height and his broad shoulders and long neck. His untidy hair, thick-growing and cut short to his shoulders with a knife, blazed white and gold in the light from the doorway. Aldgytha lowered her eyes to her lap and her breakfast and kept them there.

The girl who worked the quern finished gathering up the last of the flour from the hide, then collected a bowl of porridge from Hild, which she carried over to the healer. Taking it, the healer ducked out of the house into the yard. With an exclamation of impatience, Morcar scrambled to his feet and went after him, pushing past the girl in the passageway.

The healer was standing in the yard with his back to the house, eating from the bowl. Morcar went up behind him and said loudly, "My wife needs your help." The healer wouldn't even turn round. Morcar went round in front of him. "You're a healer, aren't you?"

The boy – he was just a boy, which only made his rudeness more irritating – turned his face away.

"Ten years," Morcar said, "and no sign of a child. You're a healer. You can help her."

For a moment, the healer glanced towards the house and, thinking this showed interest, Morcar said, "It makes her unhappy. I'll give you gold if you help her."

The healer went on eating, but took a few steps away from Morcar. As he went, he said, "*You* make her unhappy."

The impudent words produced a spurt of anger in Morcar, and he followed. "You speak out of turn! I didn't come here for your opinion on how I

44

treat my wife, but to get help for her. What's the matter, elf-born? Do you only treat your own kind?"

Elfgift, who had been hunching his shoulder and turning from him, now snapped his head round and looked Morcar in the face. Ebba, watching from the house, saw Morcar step back from the impact of that look with a gasp, as if he'd been shoved hard in the chest. She covered her mouth with her hand and smiled. She knew the force of that look.

Morcar took another step back before he caught himself and stood his ground, and even then, his mind was in confusion, unable to understand his own alarm. Yet he knew its cause very well. This boy, when he turned, and straightened, and lifted up his head, and fixed his eyes on Morcar's face, had a beauty that shocked. But it couldn't be that, not that... Morcar had never looked for beauty in another man in his whole life, it wasn't his concern, it must be something else... But he knew that it was simple beauty that had smacked him in the eye.

The elf-born's head was set on his long, strong neck with as delicate a poise and balance as the head of a deer is set. The face was perfect in its outline, in the spacing of its features, but strongly made too. The shaggy mop of ill-cut hair shone white at its outer edges where the light passed straight through it; but elsewhere had the warm, reddish colour of amber.

The eyes hit hardest. They were more beautiful than the eyes of any woman Morcar had ever seen – and he groaned aloud and took another backward step as he owned this to himself. Clear as glass, the eyes changed their colour as the light struck through them, but never to a colour that could be simply named. Too much of blue, or even violet in them to be called grey; but too much green to be called blue; and too grey to be called green. And, as Morcar shifted his ground, and Elfgift turned to keep him under the punishing gaze, the light struck from another angle and sparked a yellow in the eyes: the ochre of lichen on rocks.

The Evil Eye, Morcar thought, and felt his heart quicken its hammering. This is what the Evil Eye means. He's going to kill me with his Evil Eye; he's going to burst my heart...

But then Elfgift abruptly released him from the stare and turned back to the farmhouse. Pushing past Ebba in the doorway, he vanished inside. Morcar, afraid for his wife, gasped for breath and hurried after him.

Inside, the darkness of the low house was lit by the fire and by such beams of daylight as made their way through the open door and past the people standing in the way. Even then they did more to light swirls of smoke than to show what was going on. But Elfgift was standing upright under the point of the roof. His hair shone bright in a ray of light. And he was holding out his arms to Aldgytha, and smiling.

Before Morcar could speak, or make any move to get past the guzzling farm-people who blocked his way, Aldgytha rose from her place and went to the elf-born – and into his arms – rather quicker than Morcar liked. And everyone was watching, not only the gawping rustics from the farm, but his own servants. Morcar felt his face turn white, rigid, with fear and anger.

Elfgift folded his arms around Aldgytha, rested his chin on her shoulder and grinned at Morcar. He swayed from side to side, swaying Aldgytha with him, hugging her. A furious calm began to settle over Morcar, through which his heart beat strongly. Elfgift began to laugh at him, laughing freely and naturally, as if at a very funny joke. He lifted Aldgytha from her feet. "Morcar! It's not your wife who needs my help!"

Morcar couldn't speak.

Elfgift set Aldgytha on her feet and let her go. She turned a rather bewildered face towards her husband. "At least you know she's been faithful to you," Elfgift said, and there was some laughter among the farm-people and even – Morcar thought – some sniggers from among his servants.

"Ten years?" Elfgift said. "Married to anyone but you, she'd have ten children by now!"

The creature's unnatural beauty and its spite worked on Morcar, and he said with real loathing, "You should be dead." As he spoke, he pulled his knife from his belt and started forward to do the job.

There was little room in the house, either for attack or defence. Morcar blundered against the people hunched about the fire, who bawled, and struck out. Elfgift was equally hampered in trying to move away from the knife. Aldgytha shrieked out some protest; Hild shrilled, "The fire! The fire!"

Morcar grasped a handful of Elfgift's worn old tunic, and tried to pull him towards his knife-blade, which he hadn't as much room to use as he would have liked. Ebba, worming through the packed people, and pressing herself against the wall – bringing down a shower of mud-plaster – grabbed Morcar's knife-hand and hung on it with all her weight.

More people were on their feet now, yelling and shrieking about the fire. Morcar let go of Elfgift in order to deal with Ebba. She was heavy enough to hamper his knife-hand, but her skinny little body was small trouble to him once he could use both arms. As she clung to his one arm, he lifted her right off her feet and swung her towards the middle of the room. At much the same time, Elfgift came forward to grapple with Morcar, and other people caught at him from behind. Ebba's hold was loosened and, helped on her way by Morcar's strength, she flew and landed right in the fire.

She scrambled from it in seconds, but was already burned, and her dress was on fire. Her screams of pain and terror, horrible as they were, ended the fight. Morcar stood staring, aghast. Aldgytha hid her face. Others stood gaping, not sure of what was happening, or yelled while they stamped out flames that the scattered embers had allowed to escape from the hearth. It was Hild who threw Ebba on the floor and began beating at her burning dress with her own hands, and yelling, "Elf! Elf!"

Elfgift went to the two women, his old nurse, and the young slave. With his greater strength, he helped to roll Ebba against the floor until all the flames were out, and then gathered her small, burned and painful body into his arms, soothing her as she cried at his touch. "Sweetheart, sweetheart," he said, and pressed his head against hers.

Morcar, and Aldgytha, when she dared to look, their servants and the farm-people watched. They saw Ebba, her dress burned away, and her skinny body burned scarlet, saw her gathered up into a hold that must surely cause her agony – and yet her cries became sobs, and then whimpers, until she fell quiet altogether. Holding their breaths, they saw Elfgift holding the girl tightly, his eyes closed, as if he concentrated. After what seemed a long time, during which the girl lay quiet in his arms, he opened his eyes and began to touch the burns on the girl's hip and body, stroking them gently, and whispering over and over some unintelligible phrases, still with the greatest concentration.

Ebba hardly knew what had happened to her. There had been the fright and exhilaration of struggling with Morcar, happy in the knowledge that she was fighting to save Elfgift – and then sudden pain, quickly increasing to agony, and heat and flames about her. Her panic had only been made worse by Hild's yells and smacks. She had thought Hild was punishing her, not helping her. When Elfgift had first gathered her up, the pain had been terrible, and she had not cared that it was Elfgift, or known that it was – only that it hurt, it hurt. But then, very quickly, the pain had lessened. A coolness had come over the hot pain, as if cold water had been poured on it. Then she heard Elfgift's voice saying, "Sweetheart, sweet-heart..." and that in itself had been a balm. A great warmth had seemed to enfold her then – not the searing, burning, hurtful heat of the fire's touch, but a gentle, soft, soothing warmth that lulled her into peace against Elfgift's shoulder.

Morcar stood against the house wall, his head ducked below the thatch. One of the farm-women was quietly tending the fire, gathering together the scattered embers and trying not to disturb the elf-born's concentration. The farm-people, Morcar realized, as he looked around, were not much surprised by their master's actions. It was his own servants whose jaws hung on their chests. He looked back at Elfgift to see him still holding the girl, but holding the old woman's hands too, which she had burned in trying to beat out the flames. Elfgift drew the old woman closer to him and kissed her hands, straightened them between his own, stroked them, and then gathered her into his embrace together with the girl.

Morcar felt his own anger drain away. He even felt ashamed. He put his knife back into its sheath. The healer had been offensive to him, it was true – but against such power as this, what could a man do? He had to swallow his offence and humble himself to ask for help.

Elfgift let go of Hild, lifted Ebba, and laid her down in one of the house's untidy nests of bedding. He covered her over, and knelt by her, looking down. The girl seemed to be asleep.

Hild was showing Owen her hands, flexing them to show how freely the fingers moved, with none of the tightness and shrinking caused by burns. A wonder, Morcar thought.

51

When Elfgift got to his feet, Morcar stepped forward. The farm-men started forward too, but Morcar held up his hand to show his peaceful intentions. "Master," he said to Elfgift, "I will say freely that I am sorry for anything I said that might have caused offence, and anything I did. I was mistaken and wrong. I hope you can forgive me."

It was a handsome apology, and ought to have been answered with an equally handsome offer of forgiveness and friendship. The elf-born simply looked at him with those clear, changeable eyes, though his look lacked the force he could have given it, had he chosen.

"I admit my fault," Morcar said, "and I ask your help as a healer – for me, if it's me that needs it, and not my wife."

Elfgift reached up into the flimsy rafterwork of branches that supported the thatch, and pulled down a longbow and a bundle of arrows. He said, "I'm going hunting. Pack up and get off my land, Morcar. Don't let me find you here when I get back. Go and look for your cure elsewhere." He stuck the arrows through his belt and, leaving Morcar staring, started for the door. He staggered, as if dizzy, and one of his farm-men caught him and steadied him. To the man, he said, "If anybody else comes looking for cures, tell them – tell them I'm away with the elves."

After he had gone, the two companies – the farm-people on one side and Morcar's on the other – stood looking at each other uneasily.

"He won't change his mind," Hild said, after a while. "Once he's took against somebody, he won't change."

"We'll leave today," Morcar said. "I thank you for your hospitality, mistress."

Hild nodded.

"There's other things you can try," she said. "Nettles. Flaying with nettles is good, I've heard."

The two companies drifted apart then. Morcar set his men to packing up their goods, while the farm-people drifted away to the fields. Hild wondered whether to begin querning herself, or whether to wake Ebba. She decided to let the girl sleep for that day.

It was Morcar's men, loading the wagon, who first noticed the troop of armed men riding towards the farm. They fetched Morcar, and he didn't hesitate to alert the farm-men and Hild. These armed men flashed in the sunlight as they rode nearer. It wasn't mere leather jerkins they were wearing. They were no guard employed by a trader. In Morcar's experience such men as these meant trouble.

CHAPTER 3

The Battle-Woman

The armed men came on at a gentle jog. Their horses were big, expensive animals, and every man wore a helmet of metal plaques, with a nose-guard and cheek-guards. No mere leather caps here. Shields hung at every shoulder, and half of the men carried spears in the hands free of the reins. Every man wore a tunic of thick leather closely sewn with metal rings, and every one an embroidered baldric from which hung a sword. And at the shoulder of every cloak was a shining brooch.

What is this? Morcar thought, staring. A rich man, certainly, rode with this guard, but... Though he had never seen a king, it crossed his mind that this guard, so richly mounted and armed, was a king's guard.

And what do they do here? he thought, and felt himself turn a little cold. He was worrying for nothing, he told himself. It was only some rich man or rich lady, come to seek a cure, as he had, and travelling safely with a strong guard. But there was something indefinable about the way these men rode, about the way they looked about from within the shadow of their helmets that told him he was right to be afraid. The farm-men had come hurrying back from the fields at his word, and they had tools for weapons – axes, sickles. His own men were better armed. But these men who were coming… It was going to take more than a few big lads with clumsy swords, and a few farm-men armed with tools to deal with them. His thoughts ran to Aldgytha… How was he to get her away?

As the horsemen rode closer, they could see over the hedge into the yard. The leading horse shouldered Morcar aside and trod into the yard, sending the farm-people scattering out of its way. Some of them ducked into the fragile shelter of the little buildings. Morcar saw Aldgytha at the door of the flimsy house, and signed to her to get out of sight.

This leading horseman wore a helmet which completely encased his head in glittering metal. A mask of metal covered his face, except for the bearded chin. Thick silver brows scowled above the eyes, a golden moustache spread above a grim golden mouth. A humped dragon slithered over the helmet's crown and snarled, with ruby eyes, on the brow. In the deep shadow of the mask's eye-holes, the occasional glitter of an eye could be seen, but nothing else of the human face. It was impossible to be certain where the man was looking, or to guess what his expression was. The chill Morcar had felt turned to a sickness in his belly.

Hunting, from high on his horse's back, looked out through the mask of his helmet and saw a muddle of small, dirty huts where he wouldn't have kept his dogs. And the thing that lived here claimed to be his half-brother... The little hedge of thorny bushes seemed almost an insult to him, suggesting that he would want to make a serious attack on this dung-heap, or that he could be kept out if he did.

There was a man standing by the gateway who differed from the people who had scuttled about the yard. A tall man, with clothes of good, smooth cloth, even if a little rumpled; a man who wore a gold chain round his neck and rings on his fingers. The mask tilted towards him. "Your name!" The voice, from behind the golden lips was inhuman and cold.

"Morcar Sweynssen, Jarl."

The eyes glittered behind the mask, and there was a pause before the echoing voice spoke again. "A Dane."

"From Northanhymbre, Jarl. But I trade – in this country I have the protection of Thane Alnoth, Jarl."

For a long time the mask remained still, seeming to stare at him, but how could he tell? The smooth gold of the face shone, the silver brows frowned, the ruby-eyed dragon snarled. Behind the mask, Hunting considered. "Are you trading here?"

"No, Jarl, no – I came with my wife. For a cure. A healer lives here." It was so frustrating to be so anxious and to have to stare at a smooth mask which gave no clue to the mind behind it.

Hunting was considering whether to kill this man. The farm-people would all die, and no one would care about them. But this man's death, though he was only a foreign trader, might cause some difficulties. His relatives, if they learned how he died, might complain to this Thane Alnoth, who might complain to the aeldermen and the king... But if this stranger died, in this lonely place, how likely were his relatives to learn of it? Better to leave no one alive.

"Where is Elfgift Elf-born?" Hunting asked.

Morcar glanced around for someone else to

answer the question, and found that most of the farm-people were huddled out of sight. One of the men – the oldest man, Owen his name was – stood in the yard, but too far away to be heard. So Morcar looked up at the mounted jarl again and wondered what it would be best to say. The jarl wanted the healer. If he was told the elf-born wasn't there, would he go away? Morcar almost laughed. A man didn't come with an armed troop like this to ride away again. But would he – ? Morcar admitted to himself what it was he feared. Would the jarl kill them at once, when he learned that the healer wasn't there or – ?

"Answer!" Hunting said.

No. He would wait. And, like any hunter, he would not want to alarm his prey. He would not wish the little farmstead to appear other than it always did.

"The healer isn't here, Jarl. He's gone hunting – just this morning he went. He won't be back for – days, maybe."

Hunting sat his horse in silence, while the animal shifted under him. Perhaps, Morcar thought, he will allow me and my people to leave.

Hunting turned to the horseman nearest him and said, "Herd them together."

Several of the horsemen dismounted. One of them grasped Morcar's arm in a big hand and tried to move him towards the yard. "Jarl!"

Morcar shouted out. Another horseman came to the first's aid, and Morcar was hustled into the middle of the farmyard.

The housecarls, dismounted, had drawn their swords with a scrape of metal on metal – a sound that sent a thrill of fear through Morcar – and were going about the yard, ducking into the little buildings, dragging out the farm-people in their drab homespun and shoving them into the centre of the yard. Morcar saw some of his men emerge from the farmhouse, brandishing the cheap swords he had given them, and he bawled at them, "Put the swords down! Put them down! Don't fight! Thor guard us, don't fight!"

The men looked from him to the armed housecarls, bewildered. But, at another shout from Morcar, they dropped their swords. All of Morcar's men came from the farmhouse, threw down their weapons and allowed themselves to be pushed and shoved into the yard's centre. Morcar felt more than sick now; he felt pain, a colic caused by doubting that he had done the right thing. Perhaps they should have fought? But too late now, and anyway, to raise weapons against such as these... He saw Aldgytha brought from the house by one of the housecarls, and, ignoring all else, he shoved his way to her side and took her away from the armed man.

"All right, all right," he said to the helmeted

man's angry yells and, his arm around Aldgytha, he took her to the yard's centre. "It's all right, sweetheart," he said to her. "It'll be all right." He could feel her shaking. He was trembling himself. "I'll talk to the jarl," he said.

All the people of the farm, and Morcar's company, were crowded together at the centre of the yard, surrounded by a ring of armed house-carls. The farmers were jostled together, arms trapped against each other's bodies, with no room to move. This, Morcar thought, is no good. "Jarl," he said. "May I speak—"

The little, tight-packed crowd, of which he was a member, suddenly swayed and shuddered. A groan ran through it, a sob of distress. And then another shudder. Aldgytha pressed closer to Morcar and gave a little quaver of fear. It had started. Morcar's scalp turned cold, his face froze, as he realized what the swaying and sobbing of the crowd meant. The housecarls had started killing. They were driving their swords into the bodies of the people, and wrenching them free, and the people were falling. When the people tried to turn and run, they were trapped against each other, or there were housecarls behind them, leaning on their linked shields and walling them in – and the swords in front of them.

Morcar hugged Aldgytha to him and yelled desperately, "Jarl! Jarl!"

Hunting said, "Him," and pointed, and Morcar was silenced by the driving of a sword, a sharp-edged bar of steel, into his belly. Gaping, he buckled at the knees, dragging at Aldgytha, who babbled his name.

"*And* the woman," Hunting said. This wasn't the sort of errand where time could be wasted on a woman. Aldgytha was cut down.

Morcar, lying on his back, looking at the sky with Aldgytha's weight on him, thought: Wrong decision. We should have fought.

"Now finish them," Hunting said. "And shift the carcasses out of sight. And get the horses hidden."

The housecarls drew their knives and went among the dying, slitting throats. Other men coaxed the horses into the byres. One or two men were left with them, to keep them quiet.

The rest of the men, once the killing was finished, were set to dragging the bodies into the house. Ebba heard them come in, from where she lay, close by the house-wall, hidden under coverings. For long minutes now she had been listening to shouts and cries from outside, cries that had an edge of desperation that made her quail. She could not fool herself that they were shouts of laughter or surprise. Woken suddenly by one of them, she had known instantly that something terrible was happening. She had drawn up

61

her knees and covered her head, and lain very still, her hands balled against her mouth. Someone was being hurt, someone was terrified, that much she knew. But not why.

Then a comparative quiet had fallen. She had continued to keep still, allowing herself only the tiniest breaths that wouldn't move the coverings above her. Her eyes moved in the darkness of the hot little cave she had made, as if they might see something. Was Elfgift killing Morcar and his men? Was Morcar killing Elfgift? Should she go out and try to help? But she knew that she could be no help. The cries she had heard had not suggested a sudden scuffle, where she might hang on one man's arm and prevent a blow. So, although she sickened at her own cowardice, she stayed where she was.

Then the sounds had come into the farmhouse, making her limbs jerk with fright before she forced herself to be still again. Heavy gasps and grunts of men hauling heavy loads only feet from her. Trampling over the palliasses, something heavy thumping to the ground. The feet trod right by her, on the very edges of her coverings. Oh, Eostre, Goddess, don't let them kick the coverings off. Oh, Eostre, save me.

More heavy things were thrown down; she felt the thump through the ground. She heard a great sigh, and a groan, like a man pausing in the middle of hard work. And then a foot trod on her.

She stiffled a squeak by pressing her hand over her own mouth. Holding her breath she waited. Oh, Eostre, Eostre...

Light broke in on her. The coverings had been lifted from her head. Oh, Eostre...

Without moving her head, she rolled her eyes upwards and saw a man stooping over her, a big, dark shape in the dimness of the house. She couldn't see much of his face: it was shadowed by the helmet he wore. So terrified that she was beyond feeling the fear any more, she lay absolutely breathless and still, her eyes strained to stare at him.

And he grinned at her. She could see the shadows of his face move into a grin. He flipped the covers further from her, and looked down at her body, naked, because her dress had been burned. Then he raised one finger to his lips, and threw the covers over her again, hiding her. She heard him move away.

Oh, Eostre, thank you. The soldier wasn't going to kill her, not yet. She had a chance. Thank you, Eostre, thank you. Probably only Eostre, goddess of desire and love, could have saved her.

When all the bodies had been dragged into the house and piled at the far end, the noise of the trampling back and forth ended. Hunting went into the house and made himself as comfortable as he could in such a flea-trap. His men, those he hadn't set on watch, threw themselves down, to check and clean their weapons. Then they began to eat.

Ebba lay hidden, listening to their talk and laughter. She had settled into a state of quiet, continuous fear. Her arms and legs were rigid, every muscle braced. A heavy weight leaned suddenly against her. It was a man, settling himself down by her. Since he showed no surprise, it was probably the man who had already found her. A hand patted her possessively, perhaps reassuringly. After an unguessable time of waiting and listening, a corner of her covering flipped up again, and she found a lump of bread thrust at her. She took it and, as the covers hid her in hot darkness again, she nibbled at it gratefully. She knew that the soldier was going to demand the use of her body in return for this kindness, and she was quite ready, even happy, to pay his price, if it meant escaping from this place unhurt and alive.

Hunting, at the door of the house, peered out into the yard, where geese and chickens flapped, strutted and hunted for food. The bloodied earth didn't trouble them. Smoke rose from the chimney. From a distance, he thought, the farm must look much as usual. Only the empty fields might give away the presence of his soldiers.

* * *

Elfgift had taken his bow and arrows, and had run, and then walked, and then run again, until he was well among the trees at the edge of the furthest field, and out of sight of the farm. With no real intention of hunting, he wound in and out of the trees, climbing always, until, from the highest point of the wooded hills, he could look down into the valleys. He saw the smoke rising from his own home, and thereafter kept to the further side of the hill, where there was no chance of glimpsing it.

It was at some time in the afternoon, when the light was just beginning to dim, and it was already dusk in some of the most thickly wooded parts, that he began to notice a discomfort. It was not easy to pinpoint. It wasn't a pain he felt in any one part of him, but rather an unease he felt with every part of him; a dull ache of the mind or spirit. It was in his head, his shoulders, his knees. He sat on a slope, and set himself to wait until the animals he knew to be around him forgot he was there … but sitting, even lying, could not rid him of this discomfort. He had known it before. When he stopped trying to ignore it, and let it fill his mind, it crystallized into the words: Something Bad.

So he had been warned before. He asked himself: What? What is it?

Back came the answer: a stronger ache. Something Bad. And within him there was a tug, like the tug of a lodestone towards iron, towards home.

He stood again, and almost took a step in the direction of his steading. Then he checked. He didn't want to go home, and there was no way of telling how bad "something bad" was. In the past it had forewarned him of a goose taken by a fox, of a sudden snowstorm, of sickness in a neighbouring farm. Only when the foreshadowed event happened, and the tension it created passed away like a headache with the passing of a thunderstorm, could he be certain of what he had been warned about.

And he didn't want to go home. At the farm he often felt that he lived among the fowl in the yard: surrounded by constant cackling, jostling, squawking, ruffling, pecking, until he felt like a bullied hen, pecked raw, sore at every slight touch. They all touched him, constantly, they all turned to him – settle this, tell us what to do, stop her doing that, tell him to stop saying that, tell them that I'm right, tell them that they're wrong. Partly it was because he was the owner and master of the farm, but it was also because he had the misfortune to be elf-born, or so they told him. They seemed to expect him to know the solution to every problem, the answer to every question. And that was only the people who had known him all his life and were used to him. Even worse were the people who came visiting.

There were those who came simply to gawp at

him, and who wanted to take away locks of his hair. Why? They would, with sly, mocking expressions, ask him simple questions, and would seem surprised when, indeed, he was able to answer them in words. They seemed to take him for some sort of clever animal, such as a pig or a horse trained to answer questions by tapping with its hoof. He hated these visitors; he was often alarmed to feel how much he hated them. Being taller than most of them, and stronger – elves, he was told, were much stronger than men – he was quite capable of doing them harm.

Worse still were the visitors who came bringing sick friends with them. It was a relief to find someone with a fever he could call out of them or a cut or burn he could coax into healing itself, though the coaxing and the calling was often as tiring as field work. But all too often they brought him someone who was already dying: a woman with a cankered breast, a child too far gone in sickness, a man whose poisoned blood was choking him. Elfgift could see the greyness of death creeping into the colour of their skins and the growing darkness in their eyes, and he couldn't understand why no one else could see it. They couldn't: they still expected him to save their child, their wife, their friend. They stared at him, leaning at him like pointing hounds, silently begging him to save them from this most dreadful of all losses. When he said that there was nothing he could do, they refused to believe him. They pleaded, they raged, they prayed to him as if he was an idol, offered him money, labour, gifts, favours – and when he replied that, still, there was nothing he could do, they said he was inhuman. "Elf-born" they called him, at the beginning, a word of praise, of wonder, even adoration: and at the end they insulted and despised him with the same word, "elf-born".

Easier to refuse to see any who were brought to him, except that then he couldn't stop wondering if it had been some simple illness he could have healed, a pain he could have taken away, a life he could have saved.

But it wasn't only the visitors. Every member of his household had the ability to scrape his nerves raw with their pain. They were so sad, and there was no balm for their sadness. Their very hopes, even their little pleasures, only led them into more pain, and always would. Owen who, growing old, fumbled at the farm-women, and was grieved because they despised him. The proud child who, running to show her mother the egg she'd found, fell and crushed it in her fist, and was laughed at and humiliated. And Hild and Ebba.

Hild, so vexed at finding herself old, and so tender of her dignity as headwoman of the farm. She drew her power from him, and so constantly looked to him to bolster it, to show her the affection which would make it clear to everyone that she came first, after him. She could never understand that to do so was like waving a straw in front of a cat: it irritated and appealed to something cruel in his nature which, almost involuntarily, responded with claws and teeth.

As for Ebba, she was like a warm, living mouse scuttling across the floor – the cat couldn't keep itself from pouncing, clawing, biting. It was what cats did when they saw movement and smelt mouse. Ebba, with her mooning, her simpering, her silly hopes, was going to be very hurt by him. That was the fate of mice who fell in love with cats.

In truth, he cared deeply for both Hild and Ebba and, at the same time, he cared nothing at all. He loved them both, and it hurt him to see them hurt: he wanted to protect them from pain. Yet, at the same time, he looked through them and saw, with bleak clarity, that they were of no importance. Their pain was lost in the morass of pain that existed all around, everywhere – the pain of the wing-clipped, robbed chickens in the yard, the galled, broken horses in the fields, the hunted mice in the woods, the short-lived people in the villages. Everywhere, all around, in the air, almost tangible, was hope which led only to disappointment, joy which always turned to despair, fear, pain, loss. It mattered not a grass-seed if Ebba or Hild suffered or not, whether they lived or died, whether their hopes were fulfilled or not.

He could never separate his love and concern for them from the cold knowledge that they were of no importance. Nor was he. Nor was anything. So he bruised himself on his own nature, and wished that he could be alone, always.

So, instead of going home he turned away from it and climbed further down the steep hill slope into the valley. As he went, the ache within him throbbed with his blood, growing worse. Something Bad, it nagged: Something Bad At Home.

He slept in the open that night. It was a cold night for that, with frost edging every leaf and grass-blade, but he felt the cold less than most. And he found a sheltered thicket, and rolled himself in his cloak of oiled leather. The ache had passed from him. Whatever it foretold had already happened, and it was pointless to worry about it any more. It had been something petty, no doubt.

He was woken, by the cold, in the early morning. The first thin, grey light was in the sky, and birds were yelling at the edge of the wood. He sat up and was startled by the nearness of another person, a dark shape, crouching by him. He sat very still, staring.

He took the stranger for a man, because he could see the faint glint of metal rings sewn to the tunic it wore, and in its hand it held a long spear-shaft. But the more he stared, the more he saw, and the face was a woman's face. The tunic was so fine that it fell like cloth over her breasts. Her hair, in a long tail, red and streaked with white and grey, fell over one shoulder. Beside her, on the ground, was a helmet.

Elfgift stared at her in silent astonishment, while his spirit leaped in welcome and gladness, like the flames of a fire leaping up when a door is opened and lets in a draught. No human woman went about like this, alone, at night, and armed for battle. Into his head came the tales of Woden's battle-women, elves who rode their horses on the wind's road and, on the battle-field, spread panic or brought courage, according to their master's wishes. They had names such as Hlokk, the Shriker; Goll, Screamer and Skogul, Raging. It was their whim which decided who survived a battle and who died. But if she was truly an elf-woman, one of his mother's people! He said, "Good day to you, lady. You are welcome to a share of all I have." The stories warned that it was wise to speak politely to the elves, when they appeared. "Why have you come to me, lady?"

She returned his fascinated stare calmly, and spoke in a voice that was deep for a woman. "To wake you, Elfgift, to bring you to battle. The stead-ing is taken."

"Taken?" His steading was a small, poor place, of no interest to anyone.

"Think of Hild," said the Battle-woman.

With the name, Hild came into his mind – but then the image sharpened and became as clear as sight. Hild, sprawled, a wide wet mouth in her throat, and red all around her. A loud cry was shaken from him and he sprang to his feet. A clap and clatter of wings filled the dark trees all around them as the wood pigeons were startled from their roosts.

The Battle-woman stuck her spear-shaft between his legs and tripped him neatly.

"Before we run to the fight," she said, "let's count the arrows in our quiver."

The track leading to the steading was edged, in places, by hawthorns and hazels and thickets of brambles. Elfgift and the Battle-woman crouched in the shelter of one of these thickets, and peered out at the thorn-hedge and the buildings and the smoke rising. No one could be seen, which in itself was strange.

In a low voice, Elfgift said, "Why have they come here?" Their hurried journey back across the hill, keeping to cover, had left no time for asking questions. "There are richer farms."

"They have come to kill you."

That silenced Elfgift. He turned and sat in the

cold, wet grass, leaving the Battle-woman to keep watch.

"Then," he said, "the king must be dead."

The Battle-woman gave a small laugh. "And named you his successor."

Elfgift stared across the brown of a ploughed field to the grey of the sky, and the grey tracery of bare elm branches against it, while his mind, numbed, reeled from one thought to another. Amazement that the father he had never known, who had been no more than a fairy-tale, should have named him... The certainty of danger from the Royal Kin who would never allow... A faint excitement at the prospect. King! He could be king! And fear, because how could anyone be king, and anyway, the Royal Kin would never allow –

The Battle-woman said, "Are you a good shot?"

"I am, lady."

"Then I shall call them out; and when they come out, you will shoot them."

She rose from her knees, still in the shelter of the thicket. Her metal-trimmed scabbard clanked on her mail as she stooped for her helmet, and set it on her head, over her red hair. Elfgift, watching her, felt anger and fear tightening the muscles of his chest, making breathing and swallowing hard.

"They won't come to your call, lady."

She looked down at him and smiled. "I shall

raise the call to battle. I shall ride the roof-tree and fasten on the battle-fetters. I choose the slain!"

The Battle-woman strode out from the cover of the thicket, into the full view of anyone watching from the steading. While Elfgift scrambled to his feet to string his longbow, she walked across the track and through the gate in the thorn-hedge, into the yard. Elfgift, his bow strung, fitted an arrow to the string, moved to the edge of the thicket and took up the archer's stance, feet apart and side-long to his target.

The Battle-woman had vanished from his view. All he saw, through the gateway, was a stretch of muddy yard, and the mud walls and dirty thatches of various small buildings. Then he started, and lost his footing on the uneven ground, and staggered, as a scream broke against his head, a fierce, exultant scream that stilled the country-side. Every bird, every little animal, hunting and hunted, froze at that scream.

It was the Battle-woman. She was on the roof of the farmhouse, striding its length – riding the roof-tree – and clanging her sword-blade against her spear's head. She threw back her helmeted head and screamed again, and laughed, and screamed, exulting – sounding the call to battle.

At some time during the long night, Ebba's cover was lifted and a man came under it with her. Some of the fear that had been stretching her nerves like the string of a powerful and overstrung bow, left her. This was familiar; she could be sure of living through the next few minutes. The soldier was big, heavy, hot and, under the covers, reeked like a fox. He hurt her a little, but only because he was heavy, clumsy and in a hurry. There was no malice in it – not like with old Owen, who pinched spitefully when she wasn't as enthusiastic as he thought she ought to be. She was relieved when the soldier got off her, made sure she was hidden, and then dozed and snored beside her. But she was warm, alive, and had eaten when, if it hadn't been for that soldier – and Eostre – she would probably be dead and cooling by now. She hadn't heard a single familiar voice in all the time she'd lain there, and she couldn't forget the desperation of the cries she'd heard earlier.

Lying awake, her head covered, she wondered how long she had lain there, and how much longer she had to live. She had no idea if it was day or night, or if hours or days had passed. Please, Lady, Eostre, let them just go away. Please don't let them find me. What would it be like to die? Would it hurt very much – would it take very long? Oh please, Lady, Eostre, if You have planned that I must die, let it be quick, let it be easy, but please Lady, Eostre, let me live...

*　　*　　*

Hunting slept little, and was awake before dawn. He lay among Morcar's cushions, bored, and hating his surroundings. Dirty, poor, cramped – how could anyone live in such a place? How could anyone, especially one supposed to share his blood, be so poor-spirited as to be content to live with a dung-fire in a hovel shared by animals? Behind him one of the corpses in the heap against the end wall settled, sighed and groaned.

How could anyone, Hunting wondered, be content to go through their lives wearing such drab, colourless, coarse clothes as most of those corpses were wearing? How could they bear to live on such food as this unleavened black bread – as well chew on mud – and this tasteless mush of porridge? These people were hardly more than the animals they herded, they were so spineless. He'd done them a favour by ending their existence.

And then the glad scream – from above his head – had riven the air, had – it seemed – passed through his flesh like a knife. He got to his feet without knowing he had moved and stood staring upwards, his heart beating faster, his breath held.

The roof above his head trembled, the thatch rustled, the branches that supported it crackled and creaked. Something was trampling from end to end of the roof. Impossible. But he heard it. And another scream, and another, and wild laughter, perhaps more frightening than the scream.

Those men with him in the farmhouse had started up too. They stared at him, as if he should know what it was, what to do. There came another sound, one they knew, the battle-sound of blade striking on blade.

Ebba was jostled against the house-wall as the man beside her started up, kicking her by accident as he scrambled to his feet. Ebba, seeing firelight, drew over herself the cover that had been lifted by his leaving. Then, her terror of the night before renewed by the scream, she curled into a ball and held her breath, while her heart rattled against her ribs.

Hunting's men – those who had been given permission to sleep – were struggling back into mail-shirts, cramming on helmets, taking up spears, belting on swords. Hunting's body was shaken with tremors that ran like water through his flesh. His heart beat in a rackety, painful manner. Another scream made him tremble still more, and filled him at once with a quivering eagerness to run outside and join battle, and a weakening fear that ran to his belly and threatened to make him piss himself. He plunged from the one sensation to the other, unable to find sense in his own mind.

More screams from above, shaking their hearts, drilling through their heads. It was a sound which both called to battle, and fastened on the battle-fetters, that dreadful, panic fear that locked the joints and blinded the eyes.

Another scream and Hunting's men – some abandoning mail-shirts still not put on, and without waiting for orders – ran out into the yard.

At the gate of the yard Elfgift was waiting, an arrow already on the string of his bow. The screaming of the Battle-woman had roused him until he felt every pulse of his heart, until he felt his hair moving, until he saw every sight and heard every sound with a piercing clarity. As the first man came into the yard, fully armed, Elfgift raised his bow without thought, felt his muscles glide through the movements of the draw, bracing against the power of the bow. His fingers straightened, his fingertips stroked against his cheek as his arm went back – and the arrow flew to the man's face, tearing his lips and knocking out his teeth, striking into his throat. He fell to his knees, choking, already dying.

As Elfgift reached to his quiver for another arrow, the Battle-woman let fly with her spear from the roof of the house. It was a war-spear, barbed and hard to withdraw from flesh. The man she made her target fell with the spear piercing him from back to chest and passing through his heart. The other men running into the yard froze at her scream of triumph and, turning, looked up at her. As they stared, mazed, Elfgift's second arrow took one in the neck, opening an artery. The man clutched at the spouting blood but could not stop it.

Now the Battle-woman screamed again, raised both fists above her head and began to chant – and at her chant, the men in the yard became mad. One ran back into the house, but others ran out from the byres, and ran here and there about the yard, like panicked sheep. One, finding a friend in his way, cut him down with his sword. Elfgift picked off one who had left his mail-shirt in the house.

The Battle-woman leapt down from the roof and moved among the frightened men in the yard as if invisible. She wrenched her spear from the body of the man it had killed, and drove it through another. Elfgift's arrows flew. And then, except for the Battle-woman, there was no one left standing in the yard. The Battle-woman left off her chanting and laughed with the wildness and freedom of a very small child, or the mad.

Elfgift, trembling, laughed too, and ran to join her in the yard and retrieve his arrows.

Inside the house Hunting stood, fully armed, his shield on his arm and his drawn sword in his hand. His heart beat unevenly and fast, and if he took a step forward, then he immediately took a step back. Never before had he felt such contradictory impulses, to run to battle and to run away; and the strangeness of his own panic further reduced him. With him were three men, all that remained of his troop, as shattered with panic as himself.

"Who is it?" Hunting demanded. "Athelric?" His uncle was the only man he could think of who could, and had reason to, send such a force against him.

The three men, panting, made no answer.

Hunting, holding his shield before him, edged to the door of the farmhouse. Flinching from the arrows he expected to fly over the shield's edge and into his face, he gritted his teeth and forced himself to peer over the shield's iron rim into the yard. He bawled, "It is Hunting Kingsson who speaks! Who is there?"

Elfgift was sheltering behind the crumbling mud wall of the pigsty. He kept quiet.

"Answer me!" came the yell from the house. "I am Hunting Eadmundsson, Atheling! Who are you?"

The Battle-woman, who was standing behind Elfgift, nudged him with her shoulder. "Answer him."

Elfgift glanced over his shoulder at her. "Why? Let him shout his throat raw."

"Answer him!"

So Elfgift called out: "Don't you know me, brother? I am Elfgift Kingsson – No! I am Elfgift Hildsson and I'm here for revenge. Come out, brother, and I'll make you a present of an arrow!" Behind him, the Battle-woman laughed.

Hunting stepped back from the doorway and leaned against the wall as he thought about this answer. One of his men took his place at the door, keeping watch, his shield raised.

The elf-born? Hunting thought. But the only force he could raise would be one of poor dolts like those piled in the end of the house. They would run from his housecarls, not kill them. Filling his lungs, he yelled, "Who is with you?"

"Come out and see, brother!"

A long silence followed that. When Elfgift risked a look round the edge of the pigsty, there was a shield blocking the farmhouse's narrow doorway, and a helmeted man behind it. He looked at the Battle-woman, as if to ask her advice, but she only smiled.

Then Hunting shouted from the house. "Elf's Drop! Here's a present for you!" There was a sound of something – of several things – heavily hitting the ground. "Look, Elf's Drop – do you like my present?"

Elfgift risked a quick look round the corner – so quick a look that he saw nothing but a blurred view of the yard, and an impression of Hunting in the doorway, behind his shield. But, if the shield was up, blocking the door, it would be hard to launch any weapon at Elfgift, so he risked another, longer look. And saw round, furzy things lying in the yard. He would hardly have guessed what they were, had not one, by chance, had its pale face turned towards him. The severed heads of his farm-men.

"And I have the women in here, Elf's Drop. Will you have their heads too, or will you come out to me?"

The exultant excitement that filled Elfgift with laughter as quickly turned sour and left him shaking with fear and anger. As he leaned against the creaking wall of mud and woven sticks, the Battle-woman behind him said, "Offer him single combat. In front of his men, he dare not refuse."

Elfgift turned to face her. "He will kill me. He has armour, and I have none. He has trained to fight all his life, and I – I am good with a bow. Unless you mean me to shoot him down as he comes out?"

"No," said the Battle-woman. "You forget. I am with you, and not with him. I choose the slain."

"But – " Elfgift took another quick look round the corner of the pigsty. "He is a king's son, and a warrior – he is Woden's."

"You are a king's son and elf-born. *He* is a Christ-follower."

Elfgift stared at her in surprise.

"I will lend you my armour," said the Battle-woman. "We are of a size. My shirt will fit you." She took off her helmet and set it on his head. It fitted well enough to guard his skull from a blow. "My shield and my sword I will lend you."

"I don't know how to use them!"

She took him by the shoulders, her thumbs pressing into the hollow above his collar-bone. Her nose almost touching his, she stared into his eyes. Hers were as cold a grey as a winter sky, with a dark edge to the iris. She shook him slightly and said, "I choose the slain!"

He felt his back and his limbs strengthen, and his courage lifted. It was like coming to a fire after being chilled in the rain; like eating after a day of hunger. The Battle-woman saw the change come over him, and quickly pulled off the baldric from which her sword was slung, and her mail-shirt. Its workmanship was so fine that she rolled it up like a shirt of linen and dropped it over his head – but its weight on his shoulders was that of iron. She took her shield from where she had leant it against the wall and showed him how to put his arm through its strap and grasp its handle. From its scabbard she drew her sword – a pattern of snake-skin ran up and down its blade – and offered him the hilt. Its grip was a little small for his hand and squeezed his fingers.

"The better," she said. "It will be harder for you to drop it." Without her armour, in the dark blue tunic, the Battle-woman seemed slight. "Now call to him and offer him combat."

The quick beating of Elfgift's heart sent trembling all through his body. The Battle-woman may somehow have strengthened his courage, but he knew that Hunting would kill him, nevertheless. Still, he wouldn't run before the Battle-woman. He snatched a breath and called out, "Brother! Kingsson!" He was surprised that his voice didn't break or crack. "Why should the women die, why should more men die? The quarrel is between you and me. Let us fight it out. Let the death of one of us end it."

Hunting called back, "I don't fight farm-boys."

"Are you afraid? You came here to kill me – then come and kill me!"

"Nor am I a butcher," Hunting shouted, "to kill little, tame farm-animals. But I have my butchers with me, little pig, and they have already served up some pigs' heads. And they will serve up some more unless you come to me. Women's heads! Children's heads! Come on! You can only die once."

The Battle-woman said, "Show yourself to him. Do as I say."

So Elfgift stepped out from behind the pigsty, into the full view of anyone who stood in the doorway of the farm. He shouted, "If you are not a coward, brother, come and fight me."

Now, although Elfgift wore the mail-shirt and helmet, and carried the shield and sword of the Battle-woman, it seemed to those peering from the house that he was entirely unarmed; that he stood before them bare-headed and weaponless, dressed only in the grubby, woollen tunic, leggings and soft boots of a poor farmer.

And yet the men-at-arms peering from the house started with surprise, and crossed themselves and muttered. Hunting, behind his shield, stared, his mouth open.

There, in the yard, stood Wulfweard. At first, and at second glance, he was sure of it. Wulfweard's colouring, Wulfweard's height and slender build, Wulfweard's face. Only as he went on staring did he see the differences. Instead of long hair, hanging below the waist, this lad had hair cut shaggily short, falling no further than his shoulders. And this lad was taller than Wulfweard – and Hunting felt insult at that – this half-thing, taller than a member of the Royal Kin. But there was Wulfweard's face – Wulfweard's face made perfect – and Hunting felt fresh anger as he saw that the thing had not used the word "brother" in any loose sense. Here was the proof of their relationship. The fathering of Eadmund was marked as clearly on this thing as it was on

Wulfweard or Unwin and – more anger – far more clearly than it was marked on him. He had to catch at his breath. His sword loosened in his hand as his palm filled with sweat.

That something which was a monster, a half-thing, a devil, should hide itself in so fine a shape, should claim brotherhood with him – yelling, Hunting left the doorway at a run. It would not be chopping down an unarmed lad. It would be the killing of a rat.

Hunting – seeing no armour on the lad – aimed his hardest sword-blow, without feeling any need to be wary. Elfgift knew enough to bring up his shield – but the blow, crashing on to the shield with all the weight and power of a big man behind it, staggered him, and he went back, his legs folded under him, and he fell.

A shout came from the men around the door. They had seen a shield appear on the raised arm of the fallen boy, a helmet on his head. Hunting himself fell back a step in amazement. Then he pressed forward again – and saw Wulfweard's face staring up at him from behind the shield's edge. He hesitated for long enough – and Elfgift lashed out with his legs, caught Hunting behind the knees and brought him down to the hard ground with a clash of mail, a thud and a grunt of expelled breath.

Elfgift, panting, scrambled away and somehow,

encumbered as he was with the shield and sword, clambered to his feet. He turned to face Hunting, who was getting to his feet with practised speed.

The Battle-woman screamed. Shriker, her sisters were named, and Raging.

The sound, saw-edged and sharp, pierced through Hunting's head and locked his joints with terror. But to Elfgift it brought a thrill of new strength and power; and he darted forward, swinging the sword the Battle-woman had lent him. The sword seemed to pull on his arm as it leapt towards a target of its own choosing. It bit deep into Hunting's thigh, just below the hip, slicing through the skirt of his mail-shirt. As Elfgift tugged to free the sword, Hunting fell; and a shout came from the men near the door. As the first of them came forward to avenge Hunting, the Battle-woman – unseen by any but Elfgift – struck him dead with her spear. That made the rest of them hang back.

Hunting had fallen, and Elfgift was quick to place his foot on the man's sword-arm, pinning it to the ground. But Hunting swung up his shield-arm and, using the weight of the shield and its metal boss, sent Elfgift staggering. And then Hunting, despite the terrible wound in his thigh, was struggling to his feet. His men cheered. Their lord might yet, they hoped, kill the brat.

But Hunting could not stand and Elfgift,

swinging his own shield, smacked him in the face with the boss and knocked him flat. Then the Battle-woman drove her spear down through Hunting and pinned him, dead, to the ground. "Let us make an end of this," she said. "Your bow!"

Elfgift dropped the sword and shield, and ran back to the pigsty where his bow had been left. Beside it lay the few arrows he had left. He felt he was fumbling as he seized the bow and thrust the arrows through his belt. From such a little distance away he could hear angry shouts. A man appeared at the corner of the sty, and Elfgift ran away from him, in bounds, to give himself the time and distance to fit an arrow to the string. The man was almost on him when he loosed the arrow. It went straight through him, but didn't stop him. The axe-blow he aimed at Elfgift would have taken his arm off, if it hadn't been for the mail-shirt – and no ordinary mail-shirt would have stopped the blow from crippling him, at that. Elfgift leaped aside as the man crashed down, and stood staring and gripping his bruised arm. It was the Battle-woman who finished the fallen man, with her sword, when she came looking for Elfgift.

Her tunic was bloodied, and there was blood about her mouth. "They are all dead," she said, through a full mouth.

"You killed them all?"

She grinned at him, and blood oozed through her teeth, and trickled down her chin. "I choose the slain."

Elfgift turned, ran around the pigsty and came to the house. The bodies of men lay around its door, and he approached warily, in case some were still alive and could injure him. But none moved. He picked his way over them and ducked into the house.

The Battle-woman followed, and found him standing under the point of the roof in the dim, fire-lit room. He was staring at the pile of corpses that filled the end of the house. Slowly he approached and stooped over them. All dead, throats cut, all his people. All? Straightening, and turning, he shouted, "Hild! Hild!" Hunting had said that the women were still alive, hadn't he? Where could they be? In the byre? "Hild! Where are you?"

From close by the wall came a noise, a squeak. Elfgift leaped towards it, snatching at the blankets and cushions scattered there, throwing them aside. And there, pale in the dim light, lay a girl. She was curled into a frightened ball, and the dim light gleamed on one bony hip, on the arm that sheltered her head.

"Ebba!" Elfgift caught her up, pushing down her arms, uncovering her face. "It's all right; it's me – are you hurt? Sweetheart, did they hurt you?"

Ebba, released from fear at last, simply sobbed. Huddled under her covers, she had heard the horrible, exultant screams, and the noise of battle begin again. She hadn't known who was fighting, or why, or who was winning; and it had come to her that soon, very soon, after another breath was taken, she would be found and killed. She could think of no reason why she should not be.

And then, after an even worse silence, she had heard Elfgift's voice. She had been sure it was his voice, but had dared not believe it. How could he be in the house? And if he was, then he must be captive. She had kept silent. But then his voice had gone on, calling for Hild, calling out as if he had no fear of anyone. She had not been able to help beginning a call to him, but even as she'd squeaked, she'd known that it was wrong of her, stupid of her, to give away her hiding place, and she had cut the sound off.

And, a second later, she had been found, just as she'd dreaded, but it had been Elfgift after all. She wondered if she was mad and merely dreaming. "Oh, thank you, Eostre," she said, "thank you," and wept.

"Where is Hild?" Elfgift was asking her. "Ebba? Can you tell me? The other women? Are – "

The Battle-woman had been tugging aside the corpses, pulling them out of their heap and spreading them on the floor, over Morcar's furs and expensive cushions. There was Morcar, staring, dead. And his little wife. There was Owen. There was Hild. There lay every one of Elfgift's people: the foster-parents who had raised him and cared for him; the farm-men and women who had worked so patiently, year after year, for so little. Some of them didn't even have their heads. All of his people, hurt, mutilated, killed by men who hadn't known them and who valued them less, far less, than the weapons they had used to murder them.

Elfgift got to his feet, pulling Ebba up with him. Still holding her as she wept against him, he stood looking down at the corpses. A mixture of sadness and rage filled him completely: a hot, burning sadness that tore and hurt; a cold, numbing rage.

He hadn't noticed that the Battle-woman had left the house. He was hardly aware of Ebba in his arms. Now the Battle-woman returned and gently placed by the corpses the severed heads that Hunting had thrown out at the door. Straightening, she said, "We shall fire the house and send all these on their way. The others we shall leave in the open, to feed the wolves and ravens." When Elfgift didn't move, she stooped and dragged a blanket from under a corpse. "Come," she said. "Wrap the girl in this, and come!"

They stood outside the yard, beside Morcar's wagon, watching the house burning. The thatch was all ablaze, and the walls were catching the flames from the thatch, with a great roar. From the fields, where they had run, the frightened animals bawled. The smoke rose straight up, making a straight road to the Other World for the dead inside. Ebba, seemingly calm now, held the blanket about herself and watched solemnly. Elfgift was silent and hard-faced, still full and choked with that tangle of sadness and fury.

To him the Battle-woman said, "You want vengeance?"

He nodded.

"Then," she said, "you must come with me."

There was a sound of hooves, and there was a white horse, a horse white as salt except for its ears, which were red. It came from nowhere. It had trotted from between the breeze and the wind, and came to the Battle-woman's side. She said, "Come with me, and I'll teach you to fight as your mother's people fight. Then you'll have no need of my help." She turned to the horse and, using her spear, vaulted on to its back. Her shield was already slung at her back. Leaning forward, she reached out her hand to Elfgift. "Come, up behind me."

He moved to obey her, and collided with Ebba, who had stepped into his way. He looked down, and saw Ebba's thin, pointed little face staring up at him with big frightened eyes. Ebba had no need to speak. Poor little thing, she was terrified of being left alone in that place. She was making no attempt at dignity, and her fear flooded out, through her eyes, through the strain in her face, through the very way she stood. He was ashamed for her, and filled with pity for her, so much so that it hurt. He said, "The girl – "

"Stays here," said the Battle-woman.

Ebba threw her arms around Elfgift and clung tightly, desperate not to be left alone by the burning house, with the corpses, and the wolves that would soon come to eat them. His arms went around her, and he patted and stroked her back. It felt as if one of his own three-foot arrows had been bow-driven through his heart.

The Battle-woman said, "If you want vengeance, you must come with me, now. Stay with snivelling Ebba and all chance of vengeance will ebb away. Choose, quickly!"

It was bitter, and cold, to recognize that the Battle-woman spoke the truth. Ebba's fear, Ebba's pain was of no importance. Her pain was much less than that felt by those who had died in this place, and who were nothing now. The horses, the sheep, the scattered fowl were all suffering and, having less understanding than Ebba, were the more lost in their fear. Was he going to cherish every hen, every ewe? And what of the mice scorched in the thatch?

It was as if he and the Battle-woman shared a language unknown to Ebba, and the Battle-woman had spoken to him in it. She was, after all, of his mother's people. He pushed Ebba away, and stooped to catch up his bow. Ebba pulled at his arm and, with a sudden flare of anger, he pushed her so that she fell. Lying on the ground, she watched him set his foot on the Battle-woman's foot, take her hand, and mount behind her on the white horse.

For the first time the Battle-woman spoke to Ebba. She said, "Eostre is with you."

Then she turned the horse and, as it turned, the horse, the Battle-woman and Elfgift all vanished.

Behind Ebba the house burned and crackled, and she felt the heat. The animals cried in the fields. And ravens, Woden's birds, settled in the bare trees.

CHAPTER 4

Thane Alnoth

The buildings were all afire, crackling and roaring as the smoke rose, sending out a stink of burning and roasting flesh. The ravens cawed in the trees. Ebba could feel the heat of the fire where she stood, but it was a cold day for all that. And it would be a short day. The wolves wouldn't come so close to the fire, perhaps, but they would come. You have to leave, she kept telling herself. You have to go.

But still she stayed. She was afraid. She couldn't remember a time when she hadn't lived on this farm, fed and clothed and told what to do by Hild. Even though she'd seen her body, it was hard to understand that Hild was dead. Even harder to understand that Elfgift had gone.

She wanted simply to sit on the ground, lie on the ground, and mourn. The load of grief on her back was too heavy for her to carry anywhere. Elfgift had gone, had mounted up behind the woman and gone. And Hild was dead. She remembered the way Hild's body had tumbled from the heap, and felt for the beating of her own heart with her hand. Never before had it been quite so plain to her how easy it would be to stop that beating. She had nothing. No home, no people, and no safety, anywhere. There was no safety anywhere – except in the fire, perhaps. She should run into the fire and be burned up. That would be better than being alone and unwanted, and better than living fearful.

She stood staring at the flames and trying to find the courage to run into them. But she had never been brave and, instead, backed further away.

When the men came up from Brierley, they found her lying on the ground, just at the edge of the fire's heat. They took her for dead until she reared up suddenly as they came close. Then they clustered around her, asking: what had happened, was she hurt, what had started the fire, where was everybody?

Ebba sat up, dragging the old blanket around her, and tried to answer, but her mouth would say nothing coherent. What had happened? She hardly knew. "They set the house afire – " Who did? "They killed everybody – !" Who had? "Elfgift's gone, he's gone – " Gone where, with who?

Addi, the headman of Brierley, saw that the girl was out of her wits. "Never you mind, me love," he said to her. "Never you mind now." He tried to remember what her name was. He knew her, faintly, as one of Elfgift's people. He looked at the men with him and said, "Have a look round." They went off, skirting the farmstead and keeping out of range of the heat and flames, searching for anyone else who might still be alive. Soot and lumps of burning thatch flew about them, while the burning farm cried aloud as beams cracked and collapsed and the flames rioted.

From the pouch at his belt Addi took a length of rope, which he always carried with him. Helping Ebba to her feet, he used the rope to belt the old blanket around her. As he did so, he was squinting over her shoulder into the heat of the fire. The whole place was burning, too fiercely for them to put out. They wouldn't be able to investigate until it had burned out. There was a wagon standing outside the farm. Odd. And the wagon was ablaze now, so whatever it had been carrying would be lost.

Smiling at Ebba, Addi took off his old cloak of woven grass and put it around her shoulders. He was warm after his walk up from the valley, and didn't need it like this poor, skimpy little thing.

The other men came wandering back. "There's sheep," they said. "This goat." One man had the goat on a tether. "A cow and a couple of pigs."

"Bring the goat," Addi said. "We might as well get back, get the little wench somewhere warm."

"What if it catches the trees?" one of the men asked, looking at the roaring fire.

"In this weather? Too wet. We can come up again when it's burned out."

On the walk down the valley to the little settlement of Brierley some of the men tried to question Ebba again, but Addi quietened them. "Leave her. Her'll tell us soon as her can. Give the poor wench a bit of peace."

At the end of a long walk, after so much fright, Ebba would have been glad of any corner, but Addi took her into his own house, the biggest and best of Brierley's houses. She was given a warm place close by the fire, and a bowl of broth and a big piece of bread, and she felt embarrassed to be treated so well. She was, after all, only a thrall.

Every other member of Brierley had crowded into the headman's house, and with the fire, and the many bodies, it was hotter than a summer's day inside. Ebba felt sleepy.

"Can you tell us now?" Addi asked. "What happened? Start right at the beginning."

Being half asleep helped. At any other time she would have been too shy to talk in front of so many people. But sleepily, with many pauses, and many prompts from Addi, she told about Morcar coming, and quarrelling with Elfgift; and how she had fallen into the fire, and how Elfgift had healed her.

There was a long pause in her story here, while many people exclaimed about Elfgift, and told the tale of how King Eadmund had found the elf-woman in the forest, and recounted other cures Elfgift had performed. By the time they'd talked themselves out, Ebba was almost asleep, and had to be prodded awake to continue her story.

She wasn't very clear about it. She'd been asleep in the house when she'd heard noises in the yard: cries and shouts. And then people – men – had come into the house. She told about the man who'd found her, and how he seemed to have a helmet on his head. But it had been dark, and she couldn't be sure.

And then the screams that had come with the morning. She didn't even try to convey to the villagers the paralysing, terrifying quality of the screams, and the laughter that had been mixed with them. But they'd been followed by more shouts, and much running about and metal clanging – a battle. And then Elfgift had been in the house. She'd seen the bodies, all the bodies of everyone from the steading. Owen, Hild – and Morcar too. All dead. And in the yard, men in armour, men in beautiful shining helmets, with wonderful shields, all dead. And then Elfgift had set fire to the steading and had gone away. With the Battle-woman. He'd gone and left her. In that place.

Well, well, they said. She was given another piece of bread and a place to sleep. "I'll see if I can find you something else to wear in the morning," said Addi's wife, Eaditha.

Many of the people of Brierley sat on round the fire, talking over what they'd heard. Men in shining helmets with wonderful shields? All the people killed? Battle-women? They could hardly wait for the next day, so they could see if the fire was burned out yet.

The next morning brought even more excitement. A fall of rain during the night would have cooled the fire, and as soon as it was light enough to see, people were gathering to stare up at the hillside. Thick black smoke was still rising, but no one could see flames. As soon as he had eaten, Addi set out for the steading again, with three other men.

And he'd hardly left before into the village rode Thane Alnoth, with a party of his men, in mail-shirts, with shields slung at their backs. They, too, had seen the burning, and had come to find out what was happening. It was a thane's duty to keep order in his district. After listening to an explanation from Eaditha, they set out after Addi. Ebba was still sleeping and they could listen to her, said Thane Alnoth, after they'd seen the burning.

The mounted men overtook Addi's party and reached the burned-out steading before them. The fire was out, but the tumbled and blackened ruins were still hot and smouldering. The thane's men, wearing good thick boots, and able to wrap themselves in thick cloaks, were better able to walk over the hot embers in the yard, and through the heat coming off the walls, than the village men, when they came up.

They took it in turns to go through the ruin. They kicked down what was left of walls, and found what was left of the bodies in the house. In the yard were more bodies, less burned, but not unmarked by fire. With them were weapons, which the thane's men picked up in hands protected by thick leather gauntlets and carried or threw from the remains of the farmyard.

At a distance the men gathered round to examine the things. They turned over the helmet. It was spoiled and had lost its glitter, but no ordinary helmet had a mask, nor jewels to catch the light when ash was rubbed away with a gloved thumb. The shield too, partly burned though it was, had golden dragons and an engraved boss. "This," said

Thane Alnoth, "is king's gear." And they all looked back towards the ruin, and the corpses that lay in it.

Back at Brierley a frightened Ebba was made to tell her story again, and Thane Alnoth listened. Many were eager to remind him of what he already knew: that the holder of the burned steading, Elfgift, known as Hildsson, had been a king's son, though a bastard one. It wasn't too difficult a puzzle: a king just dead, and an attack on one of his bastard sons by men armed like a king's company and led by one whose helmet and shield were those of an atheling... The thane's first impulse was to go home and pretend he knew nothing of this matter. When a king died, murder always followed among the Royal Kin. If you were a great lord of standing, close to the Kin, then you picked your side carefully, and hoped it would be the winning one. If you were just a minor thane, overseer of a few villages, then it was best to keep quiet and hope that the troubles would pass you by.

But the trouble had come to him. If he was right when he guessed that it was an atheling lying dead in that burned farm, then sooner or later the surviving Royal Kin were going to demand an account from him. If he was suspected of keeping secrets, or of hanging back when he should have taken action, then certainly his lands, and possibly his life, would be in danger. Far better, he decided, to go to the Royal Kin himself, with all he knew.

"I'll take the girl with me," he said. He wouldn't wait for Eaditha to find her an old dress. In a village as poor as Brierley, that might be a long wait. "She'll come as she is," he said. "I can clothe her."

So Ebba, still in her old, rope-belted blanket, was thrown up to ride pillion behind one of the thane's men-of-arms, the start of a journey which would take her to the Royal Residence.

CHAPTER 5

Atheling's Gold

Ebba had spent her whole life on Elfgift's farmstead, occasionally walking to small settlements such as Brierley. The Royal Residence on its hillside, surrounded by its palisade and its ditch – with the temple complex within its own palisade at a distance – was the biggest gathering of people and buildings she had ever seen. She hadn't known that such a great area could be enclosed; or that buildings could be so big; or that there could be so many people.

A high wall of wood, all limed so it shone, and made so that men could walk along an inner walkway and keep watch, the sun shining from their helmets. A causeway leading across a steep-sided ditch to an immense gate, a gate higher and wider than most of the houses she had known. And men standing above the gate too, looking down.

Thane Alnoth's company of men rode across the causeway, and were permitted by the guards to pass through the gate. Ebba, riding pillion behind one of the men-at-arms, cringed as the gate loomed above them, fearing it would crash down on her. She didn't understand how such a thing could be safe.

Once through the gate, the horses' hooves rang loud on stone flags – there was a whole wide yard paved with stone and swept clean. And standing at the other side of the yard was a wonder, an immense hall, a great building which could have swallowed Elfgift's farmstead and all the huts of Brierley. How could men build such a building? How could it stand under its own weight? Such trees, such great trees must have been cut down! Only a king could cut so much wood.

The hall was long, so long that she had to turn her head far from side to side to see either end of it. And the walls were twice as high as a man. At either end of its roof were crescents or horns and they shone, gilded. The roof wasn't of thatch, but of shingles, and the edge of each shingle had been gilded, so that the whole roof sparkled.

The door was in the centre of the long wall facing them, and it was a high, wide double door, its panels carved with writhing, intertwining dragons, and pictures of heroes and gods, all gilded in places. Its hinges were engraved and inlaid. Ebba could only stare and gape. Such wealth, such beauty – nothing that she had imagined when listening to songs and stories had ever come near this display. Her imagination had only had huts and cheap beads to work on.

Alnoth's party dismounted, and Ebba's horseman helped her down from the tall animal. Servants, dressed in plain grey and brown homespun, came forward to take the horses, but Alnoth told a couple of his men to go with them and see that the horses were properly cared for. Another servant, one rather better dressed, came from the magnificent hall carrying a glittering cup which he knelt and offered to Alnoth; and others came forward, offering trays of food and drink to the men-at-arms. Even Ebba, as seeming to be one of their company, got a piece of bread. A king must be seen to be generous.

Ebba, staring about her and nibbling her bread, saw little of the ceremony of greeting. She was glimpsing the many other buildings of the Residence, though none were so magnificent as the Royal Hall, and wondering what they were for. She was staring, too, at all the people who darted about the paved square before the hall: a troop of men riding towards the gate; a party of servants running with dogs; a wonderfully dressed lady in a blue gown trimmed with gold fringes, and brooches of gold on her shoulders, her head covered in a white head-dress, and accompanied by a maid almost as well dressed. And more people, and more, were walking between the buildings and away into the distance. There were more people here than she had ever seen together in any one place before. It was frightening. She didn't know how to behave in such a place. All these people would laugh at her and despise her.

After a time of waiting, Thane Alnoth moved away across the paved square with some other men, who were richly dressed. His company of men-at-arms went into the Royal Hall, their captain gesturing Ebba to go with them. She cringed again as they passed through the immense door, partly because she couldn't believe such a vast weight of timber could stand, but must come crashing down – and partly because she felt she had no right to enter such a place.

Inside, the hall was even more wonderful, if anything, than its exterior. Such a height, such space! Windows pierced high in the walls shone light on to a tracery of arched rafters, and the rafters were carved and gilded too. The floor was strewn thickly with straw mixed with sweet herbs, and the walls at the upper end of the hall were hung, from high ceiling to floor, with woollen hangings. The wool from so many years of shearings, and such long hours of women's labour must have gone into those hangings! No ordinary household could have spared the women's time, or amassed so much wool.

At that upper end of the hall was a raised platform and, on it, a table permanently set up – the high table, where the king and Royal Kin would sit. A big fire burned before this platform; and smaller fires burned at intervals down the length of the hall. Again, such wealth! So much fuel it must take to keep such fires burning, to heat such a vast hall!

Tables were being set up in the main body of the hall, with benches before some of them. Other benches were set around the walls, and there Alnoth's men sat. Ebba was afraid to sit, feeling that she had no right, and stood beside them. She hardly dared to raise her head and look around her, though she longed to see all there was to see. Instead she peeped sidelong, now at this, now at that. I am in the king's hall, she thought. I am in the house of the son of Woden! Oh, Eostre!

Alnoth had told the official who had greeted him as he rode in that he wished to speak privately to the Royal Kin, to the athelings Athelric, Unwin, Hunting and Wulfweard.

"Of course. If you can let me know the nature of your business?" the official had said. Alnoth had repeated that the business was private, and added that it was urgent. He gestured to the men beside him, who carried something wrapped in cloth. He had things to show to the athelings, he said. Things they would wish to see. He brought them news.

"Follow me; I will take you to Athelric's lodgings," said the official.

Athelric's hall was smaller than the splendid Royal Hall, but even so was larger than Alnoth's own hall. He and his men went into the public part of the hall and sat on the benches with other petitioners. The steward of Athelric's household advanced towards them, a man with curled hair falling to his shoulders, dressed in a long, fur-trimmed robe of dark blue, with a heavy chain of gold round his neck, and bands of gold on his arms. He asked them their business, assured them that he would get word to Athelric, and asked if he could bring them food or drink while they waited.

Knowing how long they were likely to have to wait, Alnoth accepted the offer.

"If I gave you something," he asked, "could you see that these things were delivered privately to the athelings?"

"I would make it my business to see that it was done," the steward said.

Alnoth went into a huddle with his men, watched curiously by the steward. From the wrapped bundle, Alnoth produced four small, glittering things. He placed one in the steward's hand. It was a decorative mount, the figure of a snarling dragon beautifully outlined in gold wire. The cells formed by the wire had been filled in with shining red enamel, and a garnet had been set for the beast's eye. The steward was visibly taken aback: perhaps he recognized the dragon as coming from a royal shield. He held out his hand for the other figures which Alnoth still held, but Alnoth drew back his own hand.

"Forgive me," Alnoth said. "I have changed my mind. Instead of sitting here and becoming bored, I shall deliver these to the other athelings myself."

Still polite, but with a trace of sourness, the steward bowed his head and said, "As you please. If you or your men need anything, please ask. My lord Athelric would not wish his guests to lack anything." And with a bow, he left them. But, as he made his way down the hall, he strode out as if he was in a hurry to deliver the dragon-mount.

Alnoth watched him go, clenching his hand over the other golden dragons, and nodded. He had been right to withhold them. This steward was Athelric's man. He would faithfully deliver the dragon-mount to Athelric, but the ones meant for the other athelings would never have reached them.

Alnoth turned to his men, and jerked his head to a couple of them, who rose and followed him. The others remained in Athelric's hall, with the remains of the shield and the helmet they had salvaged from the burnt-out steading.

Outside, in the streets which led between the many buildings of the Residence, Alnoth asked directions to the lodgings of the atheling Unwin. On finding his way there, he left another of the dragon-mounts with Unwin's steward. "You may find me," he said, "at the lodgings of the atheling Athelric." Then he went out into the streets again and found his way to Hunting's lodgings, and to Wulfweard's, leaving the third and fourth of the mounts with a similar message. Then he went back to Athelric's lodgings, and sat eating and drinking with his men, waiting for whatever would happen. He didn't think it would be very long before he was summoned to an audience with the Royal Kin.

Outside the walls of the Royal Residence, within a palisade and ditch of their own, were the temple buildings. A great hall, equal in size and magnificence to the Royal Hall, housed three huge wooden figures of Woden, Thunor and Ing. A fire burning on the altar before each figure threw light

111

on to them, but also cast deep, moving shadows. Darkness hung in the high rafters and in the corners furthest from the door.

Here, before the altars, the body of King Eadmund had lain for days, wrapped in linen and packed round with herbs. The people had come to view their king, and assure themselves that he was dead. Here the priests and priestesses of Eostre and Woden, of Ing and Thunor, had watched over the king, waking, for days and nights, and had sung through the song which would guide his spirit safely to its place in the Other World. Their voices had risen clear into the rafters, had thrummed among the carved pillars.

But now the king's body was gone, carried away to its grave, to the place below the Residence where other mounds had been raised, in the past, to his ancestors. It had been a small ceremony. The king had been laid with his weapons and his horses and dogs, with gifts of food and gold, and been covered over with enough earth to keep his body safe from predators. But it would be a year or more before the tribute due to him could be gathered together, and only then could he be buried with full honours, and the mound completed.

Now, in the temple, the singers among the priests and priestesses sang hymns and spells to reassure and soothe the dead king's spirit, to keep him from troubling the living. A little apart from the singers stood Athelric, with his brother's sons, Unwin and Wulfweard. Before their father's death, they would have refused to enter a pagan temple but, with their father dead, and their uncle about to become the next king, Unwin had decided that it was wise to make themselves pleasing to their people. To be seen honouring their father as he would have wished, before his gods, would win them praise. Christ would forgive them, though Father Fillan might not. After all, they were only standing in the temple, not offering to the idols.

Athelric's steward came quietly to his master's side and pulled at his robe. He said something quietly, and drew Athelric aside, almost to the door of the temple. Unwin thought that a single, discreet look would not be thought too disrespectful towards his dead father, and so took a look over his shoulder. The steward seemed to be showing Athelric something.

Another glance showed Athelric and the steward leaving the temple together. Light shone in through the door as they went, lighting the carved pillars, and was slowly shut off as the door closed.

Unwin looked at Wulfweard, but the boy was staring steadfastly at the circle of singers lighted by lamps; and the giant idols looming out of the shadows behind them.

Unwin took up his posture of grieving son again, head bowed as he listened to the deep chanting weaving in and out of the smoke. Inwardly his mind fretted over what Athelric was doing, and what the message brought to him had been. And the door of the temple opened again, allowing clear daylight to cut through the smoke and firelight, lighting the rounds of the great wooden pillars. Someone pulled at his own sleeve – his own steward.

"My lord, I thought it best to bring this to you myself." In the man's hand lay a little jewel of great beauty: a dragon of gold wire and red enamel, with a glittering garnet eye. "My lord, the Thane Alnoth sends you this, and—"

Wulfweard broke in. "That's one of the dragons from Hunting's shield." He looked up into his brother's face, his eyes wide with alarm.

Unwin had not recognized the jewel until Wulfweard had spoken; then he realized that it was, indeed, a mount from their brother's shield. Frowning, he looked at the steward.

"My lord, the thane says he has news for you, and asks that you will see him. He says you will find him in your uncle's lodgings."

Unwin's head snapped round towards the door. That was what Athelric's steward had been showing him! Something belonging to Hunting. Whatever the news was, Athelric already knew it.

"Damn the thane! Why didn't he come first to *me*?"

Wulfweard said, "What is it?"

Unwin moved quickly to the door, angrily beckoning Wulfweard after him. The boy followed, asking again, "What's happened?"

"If you want my guess," Unwin said, as they emerged from the shadows of the temple into the light of day, "Hunting is dead."

There was a silence while they covered several yards of ground, following the ride from the temple back to the Residence. Unwin trod hard, swiftly, knowing that his own words were true. Deep within him he felt the anger, the cold, vengeful anger beginning. He also thought: I shall never again have to wonder whether I can trust you, Hunting.

He held out the dragon he had been given to Wulfweard. "How would it be brought back to us like this, broken from the shield, unless Hunting was dead?"

A man was hurrying along the road towards them. It was Wulfweard's steward. He tried, apologetically, to draw Wulfweard aside to the edge of the road, but both he and Wulfweard were startled into looking round by loud laughter from Unwin. A little further along the road stood Hunting's steward, looking alarmed as Unwin pointed at him and laughed.

"You have another like this, don't you?" Unwin asked, and held up his own dragon to glint in the sunlight. "Both of you."

Hunting's steward came up and opened his hand to show a dragon-mount. Wulfweard's steward opened his hand, and there was a third. They both brought the same message from Thane Alnoth.

"Come on," Unwin said. "We'll go to our uncle and brazen it out."

Alnoth was in Athelric's private apartment, above the hall of the atheling's lodgings. He was sitting on a stool next to an iron brazier, holding a beautiful goblet of green glass which was full of wine. He felt exceedingly nervous. The steward had courteously asked him to leave his weapons in the lower hall, along with his men-at-arms. So he was without support or protection here, with Athelric Atheling, the dead king's brother and, probably, the king-elect.

Athelric sat in an armed chair opposite him, and smiled, but the smile didn't make Alnoth feel much happier. He was fairly certain that he was safe. After all, he wasn't without standing himself. Not even a king could murder a thane without there being some outcry. And he had brought Athelric the ruins of the shield and helmet which lay at the atheling's feet, and that might be expected to bring him reward rather than danger. Indeed, at Alnoth's feet lay a very fine, fur-lined cloak which Athelric had, on hearing Alnoth's news, immediately taken from his own shoulders and given to the thane as "but a small part of the reward you deserve for this". Still, the times would have to be a lot more settled before Alnoth would feel at ease in the presence of an atheling.

There were steps on the wooden stairs outside the door, the door opened, and the other athelings, Unwin and Wulfweard, were ushered in. Alnoth rose hastily, recognizing them from times when he had been called to the Royal Residence before: Unwin, the elder, tall, strongly-made and harsh-faced, and the handsome boy, Wulfweard.

Athelric rose to meet them too, and held out to them the dragon which Alnoth had brought him. Alnoth saw both Unwin and Wulfweard look at the shield and helmet which lay on the wooden floor.

"This good thane brings me news of an attack on a steading," Athelric said. "The people all killed and burned with their houses."

Unwin turned to look at Alnoth. The moment their eyes met, Alnoth knew that here he had an enemy. He felt his back chill. An ordinary man would not have scared him; but this was one of the Twelve Hundred – more, one of the Royal Kin. His ill-looks were backed by spears.

Unwin pulled a gold ring from his finger and held it out to the thane with a smile. "You have done us service."

Alnoth smiled, bowed, and awkwardly accepted the ring, the goblet still in his other hand. "Thank you, my lord." And again bowed and smiled and murmured thanks as Wulfweard, too, gave him a ring. Straightening, he looked at Athelric. "Perhaps, my lord, I should return to my men?"

Athelric said, "Be so good, thane, as to fetch here the girl. Bring her here straight."

Alnoth bowed again, and left the room as quickly as he could, setting the still full goblet down on top of a chest which stood beside the door.

When his feet were heard on the stairs, Athelric faced his nephews and said, "There's no need to explain to me what Hunting was doing with a troop of armed men in Hornsdale."

"Offering a safe escort for Elfgift Eadmundsson," Unwin said. He met and held Athelric's angry stare. "I wonder you didn't send an escort for him yourself, Father's-brother – you were so keen to tell the Council that our father had named him successor."

Athelric stooped and lifted up the shield. Battered by the impact of weapons, partially burned, its beautiful mounts were broken, or hung from it. "What do you suppose happened to the safe escort?"

Wulfweard had been standing slightly behind Unwin, but now came forward. "Is Hunting dead?"

For answer, Athelric picked up the helmet and threw it to Wulfweard, who caught it, and turned it over in his hands. It was dirty, marked with ash and soot. Mud and blood had become trapped in the moulding and engraving. "Who killed him?" Wulfweard asked.

"Ah," Athelric said. "Let us wait and hear the girl's story. Perhaps she can tell us. Be seated, be seated."

Athelric seated himself in his armed chair, and watched as his nephews took stools beside the brazier. They sat in silence, waiting. Athelric, comfortable in his big chair, perhaps enjoyed watching Unwin trying to be relaxed and unconcerned on a backless stool. Wulfweard held the ruined helmet on his knee and traced its decorations with his finger.

Feet were heard on the stairs, and Alnoth entered, followed by a short, skinny girl, dressed in a long grey gown which was too large for her, so that from the neck down her scrawny figure was swamped in wool. Her face couldn't be seen, for she kept it lowered, too afraid to look up, but her hair, neatly parted and drawn back into a plait, was so dark a brown that it was almost black.

Thane Alnoth cleared his throat. "This is the girl, my lords. Her name is Ebba. She belonged to

Elfgift Elf-born. Some of my people found her near the burning."

"Good," Athelric said. "Girl – Ebba? Ebba, stand up straight and tell us everything that happened. Everything."

The girl's head lowered even further. She hunched herself almost into a hoop, and gripped her own elbows.

Alnoth nudged her and whispered, "Speak up!" The only response the girl made was to shudder.

"Don't be afraid," Athelric said. "We aren't going to hurt *you*." Because, his tone implied, you aren't important enough to be worth hurting. "We only want to hear what happened when the farm was burned."

There was no change in the girl. She was stricken at finding herself in the same small room with three sons of Woden. So much wealth and so much power.

"Sweet Jesu," Unwin said. "As well ask a cow!" But then he rose from his stool and went towards the girl. Feeling him near her, she flinched back, though without lifting her head. "No, no," Unwin said, suddenly gentle. "Don't be afraid." He pulled a gold ring from his finger and held it on his palm so she could see it. "Tell us what you know and you shall have this – as a reward for bringing the message."

Ebba stared at the ring. It was all she saw: the

bright ring, gleaming red, yellow and white as it caught the lamp-light, lying on the thick callouses of the man's big palm. But not a man, no, not a mere man – one of Woden's sons. She shivered, and began to tremble as if in a fever. It was a cruel joke. Such a precious thing would never be given to her.

"Here." Unwin lifted one of the light, thin arms that were clamped to her sides, unfolded the little hand which made no effort to resist him, placed the gold ring in it and closed her fingers over it. "It's yours. Now tell us what you saw at the steading."

She had the ring! She could feel its hardness in her hand. But she would never be allowed to take it away. A touch, a warm touch, fell on her shoulder as Unwin laid his hand there. She had to say something. She couldn't stand there silent in front of Woden's sons. Drawing breath was hard. Her voice came out choked and shaking. "Please don't kill me."

Unwin laughed and asked, "Why should I want to kill *you*?" His contempt was comforting. It placed her so far beneath him that she was out of his reach. He gave her the ring, she understood, because it was nothing to him. She was nothing to him. Why should he want to kill her? She tried to rally her thoughts and understand what it was they wanted to know. She was in such confusion that it might have been how many eggs the hens at Elfgift's steading laid.

Unwin said, calmly but with a hint of impatience, "How came the farm to burn?"

She tried to answer that question: Elfgift had fired it, after… There came other questions, and she answered those, stumbling over her words, becoming confused, but she answered, and no one became angry with her, no one struck her though she tensed to receive a blow… She began to feel safer, even raised her head a little, and her answers became clearer and more ordered. "And then Elfgift got up behind the woman – on her horse – and they rode away," she ended. "I mean, not away. I mean – into the air. Out of this world." She looked up, fleetingly, into Unwin's hard face, and as quickly looked down again. "That's it. That's all I know. I just stayed by the steading then, while it burned down."

There was a silence in the room, and Ebba began to tremble again, fearing that now they would get angry. And indeed, one of the Woden-born – not the one who had given her the ring, nor the old man, but the third one whom she had glimpsed but not looked at – he said, "The bastard killed Hunting!" The anger in his voice scared her.

There came a laugh from where the old man was standing. "And when Hunting was offering him safe escort!"

The big man standing by Ebba said, "The bastard killed your brother's-son." His meaning was clear to everyone, even Ebba. The duty of vengeance fell on the old man for his nephew's life: he must kill Elfgift.

Ebba realized more: the man Elfgift had killed, the man with the wonderful armour, had been one of the Royal Kin! Now she was too afraid to tremble. She felt frozen into ice.

"Here." The speaker was the third man, and he was holding out his hand to give her something. She looked up at his face – and was held, staring, her mouth open. Magic! she thought. Elfgift! Elfgift was standing before her in the lamp-light. He had come back from the Other World.

Wulfweard, amused at her stricken stare, smiled; and then she knew that he wasn't Elfgift – but still she was astonished at the likeness. "Here," he said again, and gave her another ring. Even in her fright and amazement she thought: Two! I have two gold rings!

Thane Alnoth pulled at her arm from behind. He pulled her, still staring, still gape-mouthed, from the room, and started her down the stairs with a push. She lifted her hand and looked at the two – two! – gold rings in them.

Alnoth said to her quietly, "If I were you, girl, I wouldn't let anyone see that you have them."

She closed her hand over them quickly. Her

heart was beating quickly and shallowly. She felt quite sick. Two gold rings, and what could she do with them? If any knew she had them, they would be stolen from her. If she tried to sell them, she would be cheated.

At the foot of the stairs, in the hall of Athelric's lodging, Alnoth said, "Give them to me. I'll keep them safe for you."

She held the rings fast and stared at him.

He held out his hand for them and smiled at her. "There's not the fortune there that you think. They wouldn't buy a sheep. But they might be enough to tempt a free-man to marry you, who knows? Let me keep them for you."

A husband, she thought. Elfgift!

"I want to keep them," she said.

"And you will," Alnoth said. With an exasperated sigh, he said, "Do you think I need to steal two thin gold rings from you? I'm not an atheling, but I'm not that badly off! Unwin and Wulfweard gave them to you, and I'll see that you get the value of them. If you keep them, you'll lose them."

"I want to keep them."

He seized her wrist, forced her hand open, and took the rings from her.

"Snivel as much as you like," he said. "Later on – when you're a free, married woman – you'll thank me."

Snivelling, she followed him the length of the hall. A free, married woman? Was there such a thing? And besides, she wanted Elfgift, not some herd-boy of Alnoth's choosing. Even though it seemed she couldn't have him, she wanted Elfgift, and no one else.

Above, in the private room over the hall, Athelric lay back in his chair and smiled at his nephews. "This woman the lass spoke of ... this woman in war-gear, who promised to teach the bastard to fight... You two will be too full of Christian prayers to know *her*."

Unwin glanced round at the embroideries on the hangings, the carvings, all of old gods and heroes. "I would have to be blind and deaf to have grown up without knowing a Battle-woman when I hear talk of one."

"I want to be the one to take his head," Wulfweard said. "I know you're the elder, Unwin, but I can do it. I want to be the one."

"The bastard has gone into the Other World," Unwin said, "where neither of us can reach him."

"That's not so," Athelric said. They looked at him. "Your priests are tied to this world – but the priests of Eostre, and Ing's women – and Woden's priests too – can all travel the worlds. They can find the bastard. They may even be able to kill him for us. We should consult them."

"I want no part of dealing with spirits!" Unwin said.

Wulfweard, white-faced, rose from his stool and faced his brother. "To find Hunting's killer!" He turned to his uncle. "*I* want to kill Elfgift. I want no priest doing my work for me!"

Athelric rose too, and put his arm around Wulfweard's shoulders. The two of them stood, looking down at Unwin, suddenly allied against him. "You shall take the bastard's head, I promise." He kissed the boy's forehead. "I'm proud to see you so keen." To Unwin he said, "Perhaps you would rather pray for your brother's killer, like a good Christian?"

At this insult, Unwin rose and made for the door, with a single glance at Wulfweard, who withdrew himself from his uncle's arm and followed. Athelric reached out and caught his arm. Wulfweard looked back.

"I will send for you," Athelric said, "when I have spoken with the priestesses. We will have a spirit-calling."

Wulfweard pulled free and followed his brother down the stairs.

CHAPTER 6

Ebba's Prophecy

Thane Alnoth, finding himself at the Royal Residence, could not resist staying to see the new king go to the Shrieking Stone, and Ebba found that life in a Royal Residence could be very good. There was no need to worry about lodgings or food: a Royal Hall was open to all. Alnoth had the bother of finding gifts for all the royal officials who hung about, eager to make tips – for getting one a good, warm bedplace, for getting one a seat at a feast and so on… But Alnoth grumbled and paid. It was worth it, to see a king go to the Stone. Ebba, with no position in life to keep up, had no such troubles.

But at night, sleeping on the floor of one of the

guest-halls, she would dream of the terror of hiding under the blanket from the killers at Elfgiftsstead. She would dream of the bodies of Hild and Owen, and wake in low spirits. But as the day lengthened, with so much to see, so much to hear, so much life around her, she would forget her old friends, at least for a while. When she remembered them again, she would feel guilty, but she was alive and curious – she couldn't help forgetting them. As the old proverb had it: "Don't go looking for sorrow: it isn't hard to find."

For the first time in her whole life, as far as she could remember, she had no work to do, and she couldn't help but be glad of that. There were no heavy buckets of water to fetch, no querning to be done, no animals to be mucked out, no eggs to find. She had nothing, nothing to do, all day, but dawdle, and gape, admire, gossip and eat. It was as if she had come into the Land of the Blessed.

For the first time in her life, she was able to eat all she wanted. Every day, at noon, a meal was served in the great hall to anyone who wished to come and eat: bread, with both butter and cheese, and ale. The bread, especially, was in plentiful amounts. And in the evening, another meal was served in the hall, and again everyone was welcome, unless it was a feast. Even then, though only nobles would be allowed into the feast, there was food available for the poor and the servants at other halls within the Residence. At the lower tables, where Ebba sat, more bread would be served, and ale, but also a broth made from bones, with a little meat, and perhaps beans, or eggs. And for one like Ebba, who could wander freely all day among the many buildings and sights of the Residence, there was more food: eggs from the hen-houses; milk from the cow-sheds; a bit of cheese filched from the dairy, a cake scrounged from the kitchens. Very quickly she filled out, her bones becoming less staring, her breasts a little bigger, her hips a little wider, which delighted her, even though the grey dress she had been given was still too big. Still, with the good food inside her, she felt stronger and livelier than before. And every day she thought of Elfgift. He was going to come back, and she would be here, waiting for him.

She slept at night in one of the Residence's smaller halls, near Alnoth and his men. There was a woman named Wilburga who slept there too, and Wilburga combed out Ebba's long hair for her, and plaited it, and afterwards made her a present of the wooden comb. Ebba stuck it through her belt and so always had it with her. Wilburga had laughed at her delight in the gift of a cheap, wooden comb, and often laughed at her ignorance, but was always kind.

"I had a daughter like you," she said, "with dark hair."

"I wish mine was fair," Ebba said. Fair, like Elfgift's, to shine bright in the sun. If she looked more like him, perhaps he would think more of her. She would have been happy to be more like him in any case.

"No, no," Wilburga said. "My Osanna had hair just like that."

Wilburga took her to one of the Residence's bath-houses, which she hadn't known about. "Everyone should bath once a week," Wilburga said. And Wilburga had little pots of black and red stuff, with which she showed Ebba how to darken her lashes and redden her cheeks and lips. "You're a funny-looking little thing," Wilburga said, "but quite pretty – in a funny way."

Other people evidently thought so too. The men of Alnoth's company began to call after her and pay her compliments – and not only them, but also strangers. There were hundreds of men at the Royal Residence: king's servitors – huntsmen, falconers, kennel-men, herdsmen – besides the men attached to visiting nobles. They whistled after her, and she smiled at them, pleased to be thought pretty. But she didn't go with any of them, and they couldn't make her, because she didn't belong to them. None of them were important enough to make trouble with Thane Alnoth who, they supposed, did own her.

Alnoth's men-at-arms kept from her too,

because Alnoth had made it clear that he intended to find a free husband for her, and none of them would risk angering him by interfering with his plans. Ebba felt as free as a great lady who, she thought, would be able to do whatever she liked all the time. She would lie with no one, now, she had decided, until Elfgift came back, and then she would have him. Why not? People said she was pretty. And he had cared for her, a little. He would like her better now she was prettier. She went to the temple and prayed to the Lady, Eostre, asking for Elfgift. The Lady had helped her before.

Her story had spread. People she had never spoken to would say to her, "You're the girl the athelings gave gold to." If it was a man, he might add something like, "What was it for? Would I get the same if I gave you gold?"

"Only if you're an atheling," she would say, and they would both laugh. Ebba would be thrilled at her own daring in making such pert answers – and getting away with them! This new life at the Residence was wonderful.

At table in the lower end of the hall, or in the hall where she and Wilburga slept, she would sometimes tell her whole story – and found herself telling it more and more often as word of it spread, and as people came asking to hear it. "Tell us how you came by the athelings' gold." A dull evening was well spent with a tale.

At first she told it much as she remembered it, and was frightened anew, and trembled and wept – but the more she was pressed to tell it, and the more she told it, the less real it seemed to her. She began to learn which parts people were most held by, and told them at greater length, while skipping duller passages. "And Elfgift will return," she said. "The Battle-woman promised him revenge. He will learn to be a great warrior in the Other World, and he will return in gold armour, like an atheling, and he will have his revenge on those who killed Hild and Owen. And when he has, he will marry me!" She said this last defiantly, half-expecting her audience to laugh at her – and was glad, and secretly half-afraid, when they didn't laugh, but seemed to take it quite for granted that the hero she had made of Elfgift might want to marry her. Perhaps I really am pretty, she thought to herself. Maybe I really will marry Elfgift.

Then her listeners would begin to talk, and would tell her things that she hadn't known. "The old king wanted Elfgift for king, didn't he? Didn't he name him successor as he was dying?"

"And Hunting rode off to give him safe escort!" There was laughter.

"Still, if Elfgift Eadmundsson could kill Hunting and a troop of housecarls... Well, he wouldn't make the worst king, would he?"

Everything that Ebba heard found its way into

her telling of the tale: "Elfgift will return for revenge! He'll kill the athelings and be crowned king, and I shall be his queen!"

She was aghast, hearing her own words; but her audience were happy. It was exciting to hear such things and, after all, they were in no danger. It wasn't they who had said it. Wilburga touched her arm and said, "My dear, I don't think you should tell the story any more. It will get you into trouble."

Ebba thought this good advice. Indeed, her heart hammered as she thought of what she had said. But people wanted her to tell that tale again. They came and asked her for it. "What's this prophecy about the athelings' deaths?" they said. And when she said she couldn't tell them, they offered her payment. Nothing great: a small coin, a trinket, a proper belt for her dress with a little knife to hang from it. Very flattering and tempting for Ebba, who had never been so valued before. And how could she earn these things without telling her story again? So she told it again, and told it better, with more blood-curdling threats to the athelings, and a great wedding and coronation for Elfgift and herself.

After all, she comforted herself, when she was afraid later – the athelings thought her so far beneath them that she wasn't worth the effort of killing. She would be safe enough.

Only in her dreams, where she saw herself burning with Hild and Owen, did she admit the danger.

CHAPTER 7

A Ghost Raising

ìng's priestess leaned over the brazier, leaned into the smoke that rose from it and, her eyes closed, breathed deeply, filling her lungs. Holding the breath, her eyes still closed, she lay back in the chair. Her face was damp with sweat, and the black with which she had ringed her eyes had smudged and run down her face. Her long, disordered hair stuck to her face and fell over her arms and shoulders. On the floor beside her lay her cloak of catskins, and her tall staff leaned against the wall behind her. In her lap she held a bronze bowl, filled with a bloody mess of stewed hearts, from which she had been eating with her fingers. Flecks of blood stained her dress. The ends of her hair were dabbled in it. In clumsily, dazedly licking her fingers, she had smeared her face with blood.

Her attendants, four women, were seated on the floor around her. One of them beat on a small, deep-toned drum, a sound which rolled round the walls, as insistent and bothering as blood beating in the ear. All four women chanted, their voices rising and falling and interweaving with each other, a stealthy sound that seemed to sway and blur the minds of those who listened.

From the brazier of hot, burning charcoal rose a thick smoke, which filled the room from a few feet above the floor to the rafters and the thatch above. There was a rank stink to the smoke, as of green or damp wood: it came from the herbs that Ing's women had added to the coals. The smoke caught in the throat and hazed the brain.

The audience were gathered round three sides of the room – the hall of Athelric's private lodging. Some, such as Athelric himself, and his nephews Unwin and Wulfweard, sat on the edges of the sleeping benches, while others stood behind them. All were members of the Twelve Hundred, noble, and the firelight flickered over their neck-rings, arm-rings and golden brooches. Some sang softly with the chanting, so that the sound came from everywhere.

The priestess drew a long, sighing breath and

reached her arms into the air. Her sleeves fell back, and the lamp-light flickered and glittered on her bracelets as they, too, fell a little way down her arms. She made motions as if reaching for something above her head, and she cried out. Wulfweard sat up sharply.

The priestess stood, and the bowl was thrown from her lap, making a mess of blood and offal on the floor. With a "Tch!" of disgust, Unwin turned his head aside. Athelric and Wulfweard continued to watch. The priestess raised first one foot, then the other, with her arms still above her head, almost as if she climbed a ladder. Her attendants rose, gently lowered her arms, and helped her to lie on the floor. Lying there, she waved her arms, and suddenly gave an owl-cry.

Unwin laughed. Both Wulfweard and Athelric, and many other members of the audience, turned and stared at him, and Unwin laughed again, at their surprise.

"She is in the Other World now," Athelric said quietly. "In spirit. She flies in the shape of an owl."

"To be sure," Unwin said.

The priestess rolled on the floor among the straw and herbs, and owl-hooted again. Unwin sighed. He had come, despite Father Fillan's fears of devils, and despite his own distaste, because the priestess was to search the Other World for his brother's murderer. "Christ will forgive me," he had said to his priest, "but I must be there." He had expected to see something mysterious and impressive. Instead he had spent what seemed like hours watching the priestess eat her blood-meal, prepared from the hearts of many different animals, and listening to the chanting and drumming. And now that the priestess had finally gone into her trance, he found it no more convincing than the play-acting of children. And yet everyone else in the hall – older men, sensible men – seemed held by the whole tedious business.

Wulfweard, who was seated beside Unwin, and had been leaning more and more heavily against him as the smoke and drumming thickened, rose straight to his feet, pointed, and gave a loud, wordless cry.

Unwin, in sheer surprise, jumped up too. He looked where Wulfweard pointed, but saw nothing to cause such a shout – only the audience on that side of the room, all of them staring. "What?" Unwin demanded, and took hold of his brother by the shoulders. "Wha—?" As soon as he touched Wulfweard, he saw. Emerging from, and melting into the greenish, blue-grey smoke that hung in the air of the room, stood Hunting. He was naked, and his long hair, loose and blood-streaked, hung over his white chest. Unwin, who had killed many men and seen many corpses, recognized the extreme pallor of death, the blue shadows on the flesh, the death-sweat dampening the skin. In the heat of the crowded, smoky room, Unwin turned cold inwardly, to the very marrow of his bones.

Hunting lifted his hand – a white, blue-nailed hand – and held it out to Wulfweard. The filmed, dead eyes were fixed on Wulfweard. Unwin felt his own hands drop as Wulfweard moved from beneath them; he realized that the boy was crossing the floor of the hall, was going to the beckoning ghost.

Starting forward himself, Unwin caught hold of Wulfweard and held him. The boy tried to throw him off, and Unwin scuffled with him, getting between him and the ghost. But Wulfweard fought to reach the ghost, and he was a strong boy. "No!" Unwin said. He threw the boy over his hip, took him to the floor and pinned him there.

Athelric stood, astonished, watching his nephews wrestling on the floor, or looking where Wulfweard had pointed and seeing nothing. The noise of startled shouts rose into the rafters. Men pointed, gaped, declaring that they could see the figure in the smoke. Others merely stared.

Unwin, raising his head, saw the ghost standing over him. He shouted at it, "Me! Speak to me!"

But if Hunting's dead eyes could see anything at all, it was Wulfweard they saw. The ghost's gaze remained fixed on him, and it had a chill which stilled Wulfweard's struggles. Unwin was able to see the ghost's white, bled chest and the hole, blue and red, torn over its heart. Its lips moved, but if it spoke, Unwin heard no words. Perhaps Wulfweard did, because he suddenly twisted towards the ghost and reached his own warm and life-flushed hand towards it. The ghost stooped and stretched out its own white fingers. Before the living and the dead hand could touch, Unwin grabbed Wulfweard's wrist and folded back the boy's arm, away from the ghost's grip.

Wulfweard shouted out in anger and fought with concentration to be free of Unwin – so much so that Unwin, despite his greater weight and strength, had to give all his attention to holding the boy and didn't see the ghost fading into the smoke, dissolving into wisps. Those who had seen the ghost at all fell silent and watched as it faded, and those who had never seen it, and who still chattered in astonishment, caught the silence from their companions, and the crowded hall fell quiet.

The priestess was quiet. She lay, limp, on the floor of the hall with her attendants about her. Wulfweard stopped fighting. Unwin was able to relax his grip and raise his head.

He saw solemn, staring faces, but no trace of the frightening apparition in the smoke. He said to Wulfweard, "Up!" and pulled on the boy's arm. There was no response. Taking the boy by the shoulders, he lifted him. Wulfweard came heavily, limp as a sack of meal. The boy had passed out. Unwin frowned and heaved the slack body into his arms, settling the head in the hollow of his shoulder. He brushed the hair back from the forehead, and was disturbed by the likeness of the boy's pale face, slack-mouthed and damp, to the dead face in the smoke. Was this another brother whose loyalty he no longer had to fear?

A shadow fell across them, and Unwin looked up to see their uncle stooping above them. With one thick forefinger Athelric turned Wulfweard's face into the light and then beckoned to someone. One of Ing's women came forward in answer. She knelt beside Unwin and peered into Wulfweard's face, touching his throat where the pulse beat.

Looking up at Athelric, she said, "He's followed the ghost, my lord."

While Athelric nodded wisely, Unwin said, *"What?"*

The woman spoke casually, as if the company of kings, athelings and ghosts did not impress her. "The ghost was calling him, my lord. His spirit has gone out from him – he's following the ghost."

Unwin looked down at the head lolling on his arm and felt a horror that he held a living but empty body. The heart beat, the chest rose and fell, but the true life had left it. Looking up, he said, "Bring him back!"

"We will, my lord, don't fear." Kneeling, her hands clasped in her lap, the woman looked at Wulfweard again and said, "The atheling is a witch, my lord."

Athelric nodded, looking pleased. Unwin said, "We are Christians!"

The woman looked up at Athelric and almost smiled. She said, "Our Lady Frideswide opened the road for the ghost – but it came to the atheling. And he saw it. And he followed it."

Too angry to make any answer, Unwin got to his feet, hauling Wulfweard up with him. He got his arm under the boy's legs and lifted him bodily, knowing that he would not have to carry him far before others came to help. A member of the Royal Kin never lacked for help. And, before Unwin had reached the door of the hall, he was hemmed in with helpers. Wulfweard was carried, on a stretcher of arms, to his own lodgings, to be put to bed. Unwin, following, found Athelric walking with him and, beside Athelric, two of Ing's women.

"There are songs which have to be sung, all day, all night, if need be, to guide him back," Athelric said. "You would be wise to let them be sung. That is, if you want Wulfweard back."

Unwin stared him in the eye. "I want my brother back, Father's-brother."

All night, by the golden, shifting light of

candles, Ing's women sat by Wulfweard's bed, and chanted his name, singing an endless song which told of the ways between this world and the next. Unwin sat on a bench, and listened, and dozed, occasionally rising to bend over the bed, to hold his hand above his brother's nose, or touch the pulse in his throat. Wulfweard breathed sometimes in great sighs, but he hardly moved, and could not be woken, not even when lifted up and shaken.

"Be patient, my lord," one of the women said. "He will come back."

Unwin would not speak to her, but went back to his seat. Day came, and the shutters were opened, but sunlight falling full on his face didn't wake Wulfweard. Word was brought that Frideswide, the priestess, had woken and, later in the day, she came herself, leaning on her staff, with a couple of attendants.

Frideswide sat on a stool beside the bed and began to sing. Unwin turned his back and, opening the door of the room, yelled for food to be brought. Singing, chanting! He was sick of it.

But to Frideswide's calling, Wulfweard came. His eyes, though closed, flickered. Colour came into his face. The priestess beckoned to Unwin.

Leaning against the bed-post and looking down, Unwin saw Wulfweard's eyes open and felt himself weaken as a chill of relief ran over him like cold water. Perhaps the boy would stab him in the back sooner or later, but at least, until then, he wasn't alone.

The boy looked at the wall above him, and at the priestess, and at Unwin, as if he wasn't sure what he looked at, let alone who. Slowly, he reached out an arm and touched the wall, as if making certain it was real. Troubled by the vagueness of the boy's expression, Unwin stooped over him and said, "Wulf?"

The boy's eyes moved to him, and simply stared, as if even a face was puzzling to him.

To the priestess, angry because he had to speak to her at all, Unwin said, "What is wrong?"

"Time, it takes time," the priestess said. "He has been wandering. Leave him with me. Let him eat—"

Wulfweard said, "I saw the queen!"

Unwin, remembering the tales told by the pagan minstrels, of other worlds and other courts, asked, "What does he mean?"

The priestess was on her feet, so confident in her powers and authority that she waved Unwin away from the bed, gesturing for him to leave the room altogether.

"No," he said. "What does he mean?"

"Leave him to me, my lord. I know how it is with him."

"I am not going to leave—"

"But it's best that you should. When he has eaten, and drunk, I'll send him to you. In a little while…"

And Unwin was outside the room, having been somehow guided and coaxed through the door by many fluttering little gestures. The door closed on him.

Briefly, he thought about going back into the room. But it would make him look foolish. The pagans probably did know best how to deal with the results of their own magic.

He made his way through the Residence to his mother's church, and stooped to enter its dim chill. Inside it was almost dark, except for the small light of the altar lamp, glimmering in the altar plate, and making tiny fires of the jewels sewn to his sainted mother's robes as she sat beside the altar. Kneeling, he prayed that their mother might intercede with Heaven and safeguard Wulfweard. He added a prayer that Heaven might defeat Athelric and give the throne to him, Unwin. "I will be a Christian king, doing God's will on Earth. I will bring the people to Christ and fill Heaven's fold with sheep…" His thoughts wandered from prayer to plans: the pulling down of pagan temples and the burning of their idols; the building of churches in their place. The people flocking to them; Christ's sheep.

There would be a church built in his name. He

would be a saint, sure of a place in Heaven.

Time slipped away and it grew darker and colder. The altar lamps burned more brightly in the darkness, but lit less. The saint seemed to have withdrawn into the darkness, with only the occasional glimmer of gold to show where she sat. Many times Unwin thought of getting up, of easing his aching knees and cramped legs. But that was weakness. One truly dedicated to the Lord's service would pray longer; and so he stayed.

He heard the heavy wooden door of the church creak open behind him but, before he could move, he recognized Wulfweard's footsteps on the stone floor. The boy was well, then.

The church was so small and narrow that the two of them almost filled it. Unwin remained kneeling, to finish his prayer, and finally rose and turned to find Wulfweard standing just inside the door, waiting. Unwin took his hand and drew him forward into the small ring of light from the altar lamp. He could feel the boy trembling, but his face no longer had the pallid, vacant, deathly look.

Before Unwin could speak, Wulfweard said, "I want you to grant me a favour."

Unwin waited, but there was no mention of what the favour was to be. "Tell me what it is."

"Say you'll grant it."

"Little brother, if you think – "

Unwin held one of Wulfweard's hands. Now Wulfweard clapped his other hand over Unwin's and so held his elder brother's hand between his own. "Please, Unwin. Please give me this."

Unwin stood still and silent a moment; then asked, "What is it?" in a tone that suggested he had already agreed to give whatever it was.

"Let me be the one to take the elf's head."

Unwin tugged his hand free and gripped the boy's shoulders. "Are we harping on that again?"

"But we can do it – we can! The priestess – she – " Unwin could feel the tremors running through and through the boy. "Listen, Unwin – the priestess says – there are other worlds!" Wulfweard stared at Unwin, his wide eyes catching the dim light, as if staring hard enough could make Unwin believe.

Unwin gave a single nod. "There is Heaven. There is Hell."

Wulfweard looked beyond him, into the shadows around the altar. "The elf has gone into the Other World."

Unwin laughed and pulled Wulfweard to him, hugging him, slapping him, rubbing his back and arms boisterously, to warm the shivering away. "Then the bastard's out of our reach! So let's wait a while before we argue about who'll take his head!"

Wulfweard pushed Unwin away. "No," he said,

and kept his arm straight, pushing against Unwin's chest. "No."

"No?" Unwin repeated, puzzled.

Something moved at the door, a dark shape against the dimming light, and Unwin turned sharply towards it. Wulfweard turned more slowly, as if he knew who was there.

Athelric came through the doorway, peering curiously about at the church, which he had never before entered. "There is no need to wait," he said to Unwin. "We know where the bastard is. But we need one who can follow the road to the Other World and use a sword." Athelric looked at Wulfweard.

"We?" Unwin said. "You want the head of the named successor?"

"And the killer of my brother's son," Athelric said. "I would take his head myself, but I have no talent for world-travelling. Wulfweard has."

Unwin saw, with some uneasiness, that Wulfweard was again standing shoulder to shoulder with Athelric. It was so dark in the church that he could hardly see his brother any more: only pale blotches in the dark, where his face and hair caught the light. Athelric moved in the dark, putting his hand on Wulfweard's shoulder.

"I grant your favour," Unwin said. "Take the bastard's head, if you can."

"The Cross will be on my shield," Wulfweard

said. It seemed as if he would have moved towards his brother, but his uncle held him back.

Unwin gestured towards the altar. "We should pray for success."

Wulfweard moved again and this time Athelric let him go. Side by side, the two brothers knelt before the altar. Athelric watched a moment, and then left the church.

Wulfweard prayed, muttering beneath his breath into his folded hands. Unwin bowed his head and folded his hands, but he didn't pray. Instead he looked sideways at the hairs of the boy's head shining like gold wires in the light of the altar lamp. He felt great sadness at the loss of his brothers.

Let Wulfweard be the one to take the bastard's head. Let him go world travelling with the help of Athelric's whores. If he succeeded in killing the half-thing, well and good. If he was himself lost, and his body died – well, that spared Unwin an unpleasant task which, he saw more and more clearly, he would have to undertake one day. However much you loved your brothers, Unwin thought, with pain at his heart, you would be a fool to allow yourself to trust them.

CHAPTER 8

Jarnseaxa's Teaching

The white horse gathered itself and, with a bound, sprang into the air and through the air. The steely bells on its harness rang, and it vanished from the world of the burning farmstead –

And plunged into a white fog, damp and cold, that clung round the horse's riders and muffled the sound of its harness bells. Elfgift, clinging to the Battle-woman, with his cheek against her mailed shoulder, felt the great muscles of the horse bunch and flow under him, but no jolt as its hooves struck, and heard no sound of hoof-falls. It was as if the horse trod on air. He peered down from its back, but saw nothing. The fog hid all. He

150

was blinded with whiteness – but there was a sound, a rolling, roaring, constant sound, like the sea in a cave, like a shell at the ear. And a smell too, of the sea.

The fog began to thin in wisps, and he glimpsed, beneath them, a glitter, a slide and roll of light that was like no ground he had ever seen; but was like the roll and fall of waves. And on and on the horse sped, over those waves; its harness bells clashing louder now that the fog was lifting.

And out of the fog, at speed, came – hardly glimpsed – a white deer in full flight – a graceful thing, white as the fog. Out of the fog it dashed and into the fog again, running over the tops of the waves. And behind it, silent, streaming, a pack of white hounds – and each of them had red ears.

Elfgift opened his mouth, but had hardly drawn breath when the Battle-woman heard the sound and cried out:

"Speak no word!"

So he was silent, and watched in silence as a rider came from the fog: a rider in a red cloak, on a white horse, carrying a branch of silver leaves and golden fruit. Silently the rider sped after the hounds, after the deer, vanished into the white fog.

And then the fog cleared, and cleared, and the horse rode on to the sand of a bright shore. Hawthorn trees leaned from the wind, and a spanking breeze brought the scent of land to them. And now the horse trod on solid ground, Elfgift felt it jolt under him.

The Battle-woman half-turned in the saddle and said to him, over her shoulder, "Until I give you leave, speak no word, ask no questions; keep your tongue between your teeth." She waited for no sign of agreement, but urged the horse along a path that brought them between the hawthorns and through a shower of white blossom, and on to a broad, bright plain. Then she dug in her heels, and the harness bells clashed as the horse sprang forward, and the bright land passed in a blur. The ringing of the bells on the horse's bridle became an unending din.

After an age of blur and din and a stiff breeze in the face, the pace slowed, and the horse's hooves struck ground again, and the harness bells rang, and rang again, and rang with every bound. Then Elfgift saw branches against a blue sky, and there were trees around him, thick with white apple blossom, but hung thick with clustering apples too, red and green and running with nectar from the flowers. Bees made a slow way through the air from blossom to blossom.

As Elfgift breathed in the scent of apples, and stared about him at the dazzle of light and white blossom, and the polished rounds of red and green striped fruit, the Battle-woman reached above her head and plucked an apple from a tree. Bending her arm back over her shoulder and turning her head, she offered the apple to Elfgift. "Speak no word," she said, as he opened his mouth. "Only bite the apple."

Elfgift took the apple in his hand. It felt hard, cool and sticky to the touch; sticky from the nectar. He opened his mouth again, and would have bitten, but in his head buzzed those tales he had been told by Hild and Owen: tales about those who strayed over the border into the Other World and ate food offered them there. It was a subtle poison; entering their bodies, it changed them and, if they ever succeeded in returning to their own world, they were never again at ease there, but always hungered for the Other World.

"What do you fear?" asked the Battle-woman. "You are come into your mother's country. Eat."

He laughed. Why did he fear to become wholly of his mother's country, when he had never been easy half-belonging to his father's world? He drove his teeth into the hard apple and, with a jerk of his head, bit a piece out. The juice was cold and sweet and stung in his mouth, and when he looked forward, over the shoulder of the Battle-woman, he saw what had not been there before. A high island, tiered and shelved with thick folds of leaves, and separated from the mainland by a width of fast grey sea. He said, "Do we go there?"

The Battle-woman laughed and said, "Did I give you leave to speak? But now the apple is bitten, you may talk my ear off – and I may tell you my name. I am Jarnseaxa." It was a name for a Battle-woman, meaning "Iron Knife". "And yes, we go there. To my island."

As the white horse went forward, towards the cliff, there was no sign of any causeway, or bridge, or of any jetty where a boat might put in. But Jarnseaxa kicked the sides of the white horse, and it sprang forward, its bridle rang, and it trod out over the empty air as surely as any earthly horse ever trod a ride. It trod the air above the grey sea, and plunged through the branches and leaves of the island's canopy, and so down until its hooves touched the solid ground.

"Now we are home," said Jarnseaxa, as the horse ambled beneath the trees.

Elfgift was looking about him in the shining green light of the wood. Here he saw hazels hung with yellow catkins and brown nuts; here he saw the white flower of the blackberry beside its fruit, red and black. Here was birch, holding out delicate coins of green and gold; here was rowan, blazing red against green; and ash that men were made of, and alder and willow, and strong oak. Here was hawthorn, shedding May blossom, and holly in red berry, and yew, so black and red, and elm that women were made of, and elder in white flower and black fruit. There was a sound of water.

Almost at the summit of the island, sheltered by a tree-grown cliff, there stood a small hall. Jarnseaxa reined in and looked about with satisfaction. "Here I shall teach you to fight! Get down."

Elfgift slid down from the horse's back, and landed with bent knees in thick, soft ground of grass and moss. Jarnseaxa guided the horse around him as he stood.

"You say nothing," she said. "Do you not want to learn to fight? Do you not wish for vengeance?"

Elfgift looked about him, at the light coming green and golden through the leaves, and at the forest flowers and the great trees. He looked up at her, but could see only her dark shape against the brighter light behind her, and was dazzled by darts of light that shot through the leaves. "No," he said. He frowned, trying to remember his farm, trying to remember who had been killed. It was so far away; it seemed that the distance had wiped out the memory. "Here, lady, I don't want anything." But then he put his hand to his eyes and hid the leaf-spangled light from his sight. Then he remembered the smell of burning, the smouldering of the earth walls and the stink of roasted flesh. He remembered Hild's living face, and the blackened skull it had become. He uncovered his eyes, raised his head and said, "Yes, I want to fight, lady. I want my blood-price."

She reached down from the horse's back, put her fingers to his cheek, turned his face to her and lifted it up. She looked down at him and said, "Oh, what a fighter I shall teach you to be!" But he couldn't see her against the light.

She slid down from the big horse then and, ducking under its neck, came face to face with him. His eyes widened as he saw how beautiful she was in this place; more beautiful than she had seemed in Middle-Earth. The red of her hair burned as deep and bright as an autumn bramble leaf, though it was still streaked with grey. Her eyes were neither grey nor blue, but both, with something of the violet of dusk. Not young; she was not young; but she was good to look at.

She said, "Take off the horse's harness, rub him down, and then turn him free."

And when he had done that, and the white horse had run into the trees, he turned to the hall to find her sitting on a bench outside the door, eating an apple. She picked up a bundle and threw it to him. It was a hooded cloak of leather, wrapped around a bag containing bread and cold meat. "Sleep where you please. The hall is mine."

Elfgift smiled. "When do I sleep in the hall, lady?"

"When you can fight me with shield and stave

and hold your ground," she said. "Tomorrow we shall see if you can."

He made himself a fire on the level place before the hall, and sat beside it to eat his bread and meat; and then slept, wrapped in the leather cloak. He was awake before it was light the next day, and even so Jarnseaxa was awake already. She came out of her hall and threw down beside him a light wooden shield and a long, thick wooden stick.

"Eat," she said. "And then we will see what you can do."

When they faced each other, later, he saw that she had no shield, but only a stave. She wore no mail-shirt and no helmet, but only a tunic and leggings and soft boots. True, she was tall, as tall as he, and broad in the shoulder for a woman, and strong, but still she was slight as a boy, and a woman; and when he saw her lovely face, and her long tail of red hair hanging over one shoulder, then his arms drooped, and the shield and stave drooped with them.

"Lady," he said, "I don't want to hurt you."

"You won't hurt me," she said. "Guard yourself!" And she came at him with the stave.

He put up the shield, thinking to turn the blow aside, but she struck him with such weight that he went backwards and crumpled under it. And while he lay on the ground, she lambasted him with the stave, so the crashes rang about the forest and frightened up the birds with wing-clappings and screeches.

"Now," she said, leaning on the stave and watching him huddle under his shield while he felt at his bruises, "remember never to think lightly of an opponent. Up!"

He got to his feet and she came at him again. This time he tried hard to guard himself, but when his shield was up to fend off a blow from above, she knocked his legs from under him instead. Or she changed her swing and bruised the ribs of his unguarded side.

"Slow!" she cried. "Slow!"

She made him furious, and he threw his shield aside and tried to beat her down with his own stave, to pay her back in pain the pain she had caused him. But she danced out of reach, and laughed, and numbed his arm and his leg with blows, and beat him across the shoulders when he fell. Then she offered him her hand to help him up. "I am sorry," she said. "But you are going to have to fight; it is the weird woven for you. And these fights that are coming to you will not be with sticks, but with edged blades. You have much to learn; but you will do better."

And she went into the hall and fetched a flask of salve, with which she rubbed his back and sides, saying it would ease the bruises; which it did. The bruises which should have blackened by the next morning, making every movement painful, were hardly yellow.

Every day was spent in running races around the woodland paths and in practising with the shield and staves. Jarnseaxa made him practise and practise the blocking of her blows with the shield, even rousing him in the night and making him practise again by moonlight, when he was bleary with weariness. She practised him until she could not get a blow past his shield, try as she might.

"Now I can sleep in the hall!" he cried – and she swept his legs from under him.

"Not yet!" And then she practised him in leaping above blows aimed at his legs, and in guarding himself from blows aimed at him when he was on the ground. But days went by, and days more, and still more days, and then came the day when she tried, and failed, to land a blow, or trip him, and when he drove her to her knees. She threw down her shield and stave and spread her arms to signal that she admitted defeat, and cried, "Tonight you sleep in the hall!"

Yet during all these long days of practice, neither the days nor the nights had grown longer, and the trees of the forest still bloomed and fruited together, and Elfgift could not tell how long he had been there, on Jarnseaxa's island.

The hall was small and simple. To one side of

the entrance passage was a byre, where pigs sheltered at night; to the other side a small room with sleeping benches, and a fire, and a big closet bed at one end.

"You will sleep by the fire," Jarnseaxa said. "The bed is mine."

Elfgift threw his leather cloak down on the sleeping bench, and grinned and said, "When shall I sleep in the bed, lady?"

She sat down on the other bench, and said, "When you can have your hair braided into many tiny braids, and run through this forest, pursued by thirty armed men, and not be caught, nor wounded, nor let one braid be unravelled; when you can leap over a stick held as high as your head, and run under one held as low as your knee, and never break stride; and when, on your knees, and armed with only a shield and a stave, you can defend yourself against thirty armed men and never take a wound – then Elfgift, my beautiful boy, you may sleep in my bed."

Elfgift sat on his bench, and stared, and then pulled the leather cloak straight.

"I had better get comfortable here," he said.

She laughed, and threw him the leather bag that was always full of bread.

He had thought she baked the bread but, now that he lived in the hall, he learned that, every morning, a raven landed on the roof of the hall, croaked, and dropped the bag in front of the door. And it became his task, whenever they needed meat, to kill one of the pigs. Its hairy skin was to be carefully cut from the carcass, and laid aside; and the bones were never to be broken. Once picked clean, they were to be placed on the pig-skin and wrapped up, and placed outside. The next day's sunrise returned the pig to life, and it trotted off to feed with the rest of the herd. He had wondered at this; but then shrugged and said to himself, "I am come into my mother's country."

His training went on; and he ate the fruit of the Other World, ate the flesh of the fish that swam in its seas and streams, and of the birds that flew in its air; the game that wandered its woods. That food changes those who eat it; and he was glad of it. He had a score to settle in his father's world; but once that was done, he would return, for ever, to his mother's world, where the apple blossomed and fruited in the same unchanging season.

Jarnseaxa would take a bundle of sticks from a corner of her hall and cast them into the air. As they fell, they would become a band of thick-set men, armed with spears and swords. Elfgift would run from them, or fight them; and desperate fighting it was, until Jarnseaxa called out the words that turned the warriors to sticks once more. Jarnseaxa had salves that healed any wound he took, but the wounds still hurt, and shamed him; and any wound, even the slightest scratch, meant that he still slept on the bench – and the Battle-woman seemed more beautiful to him day by day.

But his body was strengthening, and his mind was bent to success, and in time he could evade the men – though Jarnseaxa added more and more to the band that chased him – could evade them all day, and never take a scratch or a bruise. And after more time, he could defend himself from them, on his knees, armed only with a shield and a stave, and they never landed a blow.

Jarnseaxa began to braid up his hair, which had grown long, like the hair of an atheling. Into innumerable fine braids she plaited it, and after the chase was done, she would ruffle through his hair and say, "Here is a braid undone – here another. You must have caught it on a twig. No, I sleep alone tonight."

So not only must he evade the men, and their weapons, but he must duck and twist and fend off branches – and still see the spear's flight, the sword's swing… For a while, Jarnseaxa needed her salve again as, intent on keeping his hair in braids, he was struck by one weapon or another. But in time he learned even this quickness, and there came a day when Jarnseaxa could not find an unravelled braid in his hair. "But tomorrow?" she said. The end of the next day came, and every braid was in place; but, though he could leap a branch held as high as his head, he could not run under one as low as his knee – not without breaking stride. But on the third day, his braids were in place; and he leaped the high branch, and ran under the low branch, and all without breaking stride.

Jarnseaxa stepped into his arms, embraced him warmly, and kissed him, and spread his long braided hair around her own shoulders.

"Now you must wear the hero-braids," she said, stroking his face.

That night they were in the big bed together, and Elfgift felt himself weak with wonder and love, for never had any man such a lady as this. She was everything, a whole world to him. She was beautiful; and she was soft to touch. She was gentle and loving and dear as any mother or sweetheart; and yet fierce and strong and murderous; strict as a sergeant. When she was kind, it was a blessing; yet she was honest as a smack in the face, and her praise could not be easily won. Once she had fastened the fear-fetters on Hunting's men. Now he felt love's fetters fasten around him.

He did not ask why she was so eager for the people of a small steading to be avenged that she had brought him out of Middle-Earth to this place, and trained him to take that vengeance. He did not care, so long as he could be with her. Though he had learned so much, and his hair had grown so long, he did not wonder how long he had been in the Other World. He did not care; he did not wish to be anywhere else.

He let her braid the long, fine hero-braids into his hair at either side of his face; and he plaited them into her hair; and he waited for her to say what they would do. He didn't care. Whatever she wished for, he wished for. He was hers.

CHAPTER 9

Into the Other World

Wulfweard stood in the centre of the room. His long hair had been drawn back and bound into a tail down his back. The light of the candles shifted over the many grey iron links in the heavy mail-shirt that hung from his shoulders, and shone with smooth intensity on the polished round of the masked helmet he held under his arm. A sword was slung from his shoulder on an embroidered baldric, and at his other side shone the hilt of a seax, a long knife. At his back was slung a light shield, marked with the sign of the Cross. He was armed for revenge, a duty three times demanded: for the life of a member of the Twelve Hundred, a life that twelve hundred ounces of silver had never been enough to buy; for the life of a member of the Royal Kin, whose blood-price was paid in countries; and, most urgent of all, for the life of a brother. Wulfweard was proud that the duty had been granted to him, and braced his shoulders under the weight of the iron shirt. The journey ahead of him led out of this world and into one where there was no telling what dangers he might meet, alone – but he would let no one see that he was afraid.

Frideswide knelt at one side of the room, swaying as she chanted. Her women, gathered around her, beat drums and chanted. The fire burning in the brazier drew a scent of wood from the panelled walls, and released a drowsy smoke. The drums beat on: the priestess would "fly on the wings of the drum". Athelric was there too, seated in his armed chair. Unwin was beside him, on a stool. Frideswide had asked that Unwin, as an unbeliever, should not speak, at any time.

"My brother is also a – Believer," Unwin had said.

At that, Frideswide had turned her head a little aside and smiled.

The chamber was Athelric's private room, above his hall. As Wulfweard listened to the interweaving of chanting and drumming, he watched the candlelight move over the intertwining dragons carved on the wall panels. And there was

Tiw, the ancient god, displaying the stump of his wrist, where the Wolf had bitten off his hand. There was Ing's sacred ship setting sail – and there the battle-women rode beneath the linked triangles that represented the battle-fetters. He found his head drooping and his sight blurring.

Ing's women came to him and, taking his helmet from him, helped him to lie on the floor. One put a cushion under his head; another placed the helmet by his side. He found the hilt of his sword and grasped it. The drumming, the singing, the smoke, would lift his spirit out of this world and carry it into another. There he would find his spirit body dressed in armour, with his sword in his hand. When he had found it strange, Frideswide had asked him, "Have you never dreamed and, in the dream, found water wet to touch and stone hard? Have you never, in a dream, used a sword, or taken a blow on a shield?"

He had, many times.

"Where do you think you go, in dreams, but into another world?" she asked. "But now you will be guided by me, instead of drifting like thistledown. When you wake, in that Other World, you will have no feeling of having left your body behind. But eat nothing and drink nothing. Drink one drop, eat one crumb, and I can never call you back."

Athelric, leaning on his chair's arm as he

supported his head on his hand, felt his own heart slowing to the rhythm of the drum's beat. Unwin, beside him, shook his head, trying to clear it. He tried to blow the smoke out of his lungs, angry that the heathen magic should be overcoming him. A darkness came over his eyes, and he blinked, fearing that his sight was going. But it was only that Ing's women had snuffed some of the candles, and the shadows had moved out from the corners of the room.

The few candles still lit shed their most intense light on the figure lying on the floor, picking out the brightest strands of his hair, the gold in the embroidery of the baldric, bringing points of white light from the shield and helmet laid beside him. He was laid out as if in his own grave, with his grave-goods around him. As if for a pagan burial, Unwin noted, not a Christian.

The sound of the drum, and of the deep-throated humming of the priestess, boomed softly from the wooden walls, thrummed under the thatch, set even the candlelight quivering. Athelric's head sank, his eyes closed again however often he opened them, and when Wulfweard wavered and dissolved into the gauzy light, he thought only that he was drowsing. It was the saw-edged cry of fright from one of the women, and the shout from Unwin, that brought up his head with a jerk and opened his eyes wide.

Wulfweard no longer lay on the floor. A cushion, imprinted with the shape of the boy's head, still lay in place. The helmet, shield and sword were gone. Unsteadily Athelric rose from his chair and went forward, blundered to one knee, and put his hand on the cushion. The hollow was still warm, and the rough skin of his fingers snagged up a long fair hair. Athelric was silent, and felt a great silence inside himself, of awe and wonder. He looked across the room at his priestess, Frideswide, who lay slumped in a heap, her breathing loud and rough. Her open mouth dribbled on to a gold-embroidered cushion. Several of her women bent over her. Others stared at the place where Wulfweard had lain.

Unwin had also risen, and loomed above his uncle, a black shape against the candlelight, smoke swirling around him. He turned his head, looking from one corner of the room to another, looking high and low, trying to find his brother anywhere.

Athelric, still bleary, groped his way back to his chair, and sat heavily. He looked from Ing's women to Ing's sacred ship and Tiw's stump carved on his walls, while his mind groped as his hands had done, without finding anything to help him understand. That a spirit could leave its body and travel to another world, he devoutly believed: but that a body, flesh, bone and blood, could be taken with its spirit was surely impossible. Again and again his eyes returned to that imprint in the cushion.

Unwin, leaning above him, said, "Now you are rid of two brother's-sons, Uncle."

One clear thought formed in Athelric's mind. It was: But I am rid of the wrong brother's-son.

Wulfweard had drowsed to the drumming and the singing of the women, sinking deep towards sleep, and deeper than sleep – and then had woken as his heart shrank in pain, as if he was rooted to his own world at his heart, and he was being torn from it. Gasping for breath, he tried to rise from sleep, but floundered – the world turned – and he came, as through water, and upright, on his feet and no longer lying down, into another place.

The candlelight wavered, water-rippled, but through its shifting he saw a small chamber, lit with the warm light of fire and lamp. Opposite him, filling his eyes and the whole side of the room, was a loom. He sensed someone – someone at the edge of his vision – but he looked only at the loom.

The warp and weft was white, and blue, and red and yellow. Soft and slippery, and dripping reeking blood, the threads were of guts and sinew. The weights that pulled the warp straight were severed heads with sagging blue lips and drooping eyelids. Warp and weft were parted by a great, grey spear, and the shuttle that dragged through the warp was a thigh bone.

A woman's voice spoke, the voice of that figure at the edge of his sight. "I am weaving the warweb." The spear parted the soft threads, the shuttle flew, and he saw a fine woollen cloth, woven with an angular pattern of men with raised axes, in red and yellow and blue. The loom weights were round, pierced stones. He put a hand to his dizzied head and could not be sure that he had ever seen anything else.

"Wulfweard, Atheling!" said the woman's voice. "You are welcome."

He looked at her for the first time, and was taken aback by her beauty. Red hair hung over her shoulders, finely streaked with grey, red-gold inlaid with silver. Round her neck was a thick ring of gold, and at her shoulders two oval golden brooches, with beads of garnet and amber strung between them. Her small waist was bound with a belt of gold, from which hung scissors, and keys, and a long knife, a seaxa, like the one at his side. She was smiling. "Did you think," she said, "to sneak into my world, into my hall, unnoticed, like a mouse into a pantry?" Still smiling, she left the loom and came towards him, her arms held out, and she would have embraced him if he had not flinched from her, expecting her to be bloodied from her weaving. But she was clean and beautiful, and her weaving was only of wool. So he let her catch him in her arms, and press her softness against him, and kiss his cheek. "Such beautiful young men as you are always welcome to the benches in my hall," she said. "Let me find you a seat, and bring you bread and drink –" He pulled away from her, and she laughed. "Oh, you think you won't eat or drink in *my* hall." She leaned close to him again, and whispered in his ear, so that her breath tickled against his skin. "I know why you have come here, and whose head you wish to take. Well, you shall have your chance. You have not long to wait."

From somewhere outside the hall there came an uproar of shouting and cheering. She raised her head, listening. "No," she said, "not long to wait." She took his hand and led him towards a curtained door. "Come and see a contest, and then fight your own, if you have the courage. Do you have the courage?"

"I had the courage to come here!"

"But perhaps you have used it all, and have none left?" she said; and led him through the door into a crowded and noisy hall.

CHAPTER 10

Woden's Promise

Elfgift was woken by cold, and by the flat, harsh cry of a crow. He sat, and found himself in the open air, in the cold grey dusk of early morning. He looked about, but the dark shape of Jarnseaxa's hall was not there, nor the dark shapes of familiar trees. Nor was the sound of the wind in the trees the sound he had grown used to; nor was there the sound of the sea around Jarnseaxa's island. The crow croaked again.

He got to his feet, and found that he was dressed in a limp tunic of homespun wool, grown soft by much use; and that he was barelegged and barefoot, like a slave. It was cold. He hugged himself, and rubbed the cold toes of one foot against the other calf.

His weapons and armour were gone. He hadn't even a knife. He poked about in the leaf-mould where he had been lying, and found nothing – not a flask, not a loaf, not a leather cloak to keep the rain off.

He waited, shivering, until the dusk lightened, and then explored a little, but still it was so hard to see in the dim light under the trees that only the quickness Jarnseaxa had taught him kept him from bashing his head on branches and blundering into thorn thickets.

He was in a strange forest. Not one tree, not one path did he know. He stopped at a brown stream, where foxgloves leaned over the water, drank, and tried to remember how he had come there. But he could only remember falling asleep beside Jarnseaxa, with his arms around her, in the warmth of the bed-closet.

As the daylight strengthened, and showed him the many trees, with their litter of leaves and fallen branches around them, the tangles of low bushes, the stumps eaten by fungi and strewn round with rotten wood; as cold water dripped on him, and his bare feet floundered in cold, slippery leaf-litter, then, as he shivered, he began to ask himself: Had there ever been a beautiful Battle-woman and a warm bed? Or had that been the dream of a hungry slave?

Then he looked down at himself and saw the

strong muscles in his bare legs. He held out his arms and hands, and saw the muscles and callouses of weapon-training. And beside his face hung the hero-braids which Jarnseaxa had plaited there.

So, he had been cast out. He had come into his mother's country but, it seemed, he was no more wanted there than he had been in his father's world.

The daylight was brightening, and the leaves showed green. To warm himself, and to ease his anger, he ran, balanced on his hands, turned somersaults. He ran through the forest, avoiding every branch and briar that would trip or catch him. He leaped as high as his own head, and ducked as low as his own knee, and knew that he had truly learned these things, and not merely dreamed of learning them. But the lady for whom he had learned these things no longer wanted him.

Why? Why was he abandoned, turned out with nothing? What had he done? He stopped, and sat in the wet leaf-litter close beside a forest ride. A blackthorn foamed white and green close by him, and rowan blazed green and red-berried. An apple had red fruit among its green leaves and white blossom. He looked at none of them.

A sound of hoof-beats roused him, and a tremble of hoof-beats through the ground. Through the trees came a party of young men on horseback.

They all wore gold rings about their necks, and gold brooches at their shoulders. Bows were on their shoulders, and hounds ran about the horses' feet. They saw Elfgift sitting by the track, and they reined in and studied him, while their hounds ran up to him and thrust their wet noses hard into his face and against his chest.

Elfgift had to stand before the dogs over-whelmed him, and then they leapt about him, putting heavy paws on his shoulders and chest, and licking his face. One of the young riders, leaning on his saddle-bow, said, "What sort of slave wears hero-braids?"

Another said, "A strong one, certainly! You'd get a day's work out of him! Who will bid?"

"A runaway," said a third, "come here in nothing but that sorry shirt."

"But the hero-braids! Look, he wears hero-braids!"

And one of the young men brought his horse close to Elfgift, peered down at him and said, "Why have you woven those hero-braids into your hair, you bare-arsed scarecrow?"

A great hound had its paws on Elfgift's shoulders, and he was striving to hold its weight off him. As it licked his neck and face, he looked up at the horseman and said, "The Lady Jarnseaxa braided my hair, after I had earned the braids."

The young man called to his companions,

laughing, "He says he has earned the braids!"

They laughed too. None of them, Elfgift saw, wore the braids.

"*He* has earned the braids!"

"Where is your neck-ring, hero?"

"Have you eaten your horse?"

"Given away your weapons, have you?"

"No, no! It's true – he is a great hero, of a great lineage! His name is Slave, son of Thrall, son of Churl, son of Bent-Back, son of –"

It seemed to Elfgift that they made little of Jarnseaxa, and laughed at the training she had given him, doubted her, and even though she had deserted him, that enraged him. Perhaps he was even angrier than he would have been if she had still been with him. He pushed the dog away from him and, turning, said to them all, "Give me a stick, and I'll defend myself against you all – and break your heads open too!"

"He's mad! A mad slave!" said one to the others, and all laughed, and turned their big, hot horses close around him, so that he was jostled by them, knocked aside by hard horse muscle.

"Perhaps his master threw him out. Who wants a mad slave?"

"Not here!" said another. "If you want to prove your right to the braids, come to the hall! It'll make an evening's entertainment."

And the young men rode on along the forest

track, with their dogs following. Elfgift followed too, because he was angry, and wanted to make them take back their words. And because he was angry, and wanted to hurt someone.

It was a short way he had to follow the young men – it seemed he had hardly taken a step or two when the country changed about them, and instead of making their way through forest, they were climbing a hillside from which every tree had been cleared. Elfgift turned and looked back, and saw the forest below them in the valley, as if they had come faster and further than he remembered.

Ahead of them, at the crown of the hill, was a tall palisade, plastered white so that it gleamed. Through the gate of this palisade the young men rode, calling out to the guards, who lowered their weapons and allowed Elfgift to follow them in on foot. Servants came running to take the horses, and the young men went into the hall, their dogs clustering around them. One looked back and beckoned Elfgift to follow, as he might have called in a wandering hound.

It was the hall of a great lord, even of a king, for never had Elfgift seen so many benches and, on the benches, so many young men – and, on the white-plastered walls, so many weapons. And a thing most remarkable – the central pillar of the house, holding up the high, shadowed roof, was a living tree. And sunk to the hilt in that tree was a sword – the light from the open door brought a faint gleam from its pommel.

One of the young men took from a friend a shield that was being polished and, drawing his long knife, stepped up on a bench and beat the knife-blade on the shield. The noise rang through the hall, and all faces turned towards him, and the noise of laughter and argument stopped.

"Look here!" cried the young man, pointing at Elfgift with the knife. "Here we have a challenger! Here is one who claims a right to wear the hero-braids!"

The men who crowded the hall began to rise from their places and to gather close around Elfgift, staring.

"*This* is a hero?" they said. "This barefoot slave?"

"What is your blood-price?" they asked Elfgift. "A bowl of stew?"

The speaker struck the shield with his knife again. "He is willing to prove his right! Who will fight him? Who will meet this fearsome challenger in combat? Come on now!"

The men began to back away, turning aside and laughing, shaking their heads. "Raise a weapon against *him*?"

"I would dishonour my shield and my sword."

Their contempt, their smiling faces, infuriated Elfgift, but he set his teeth and held on to his temper. A furious man is a bad fighter.

"I hear cowards making excuses," he said. "Among all of you here, isn't there one who will fight me?"

They laughed at him again, and called, "Who will brawl with the herd-boy? Step forward! Who will roll in the rushes with the slave?"

From somewhere in the crowd came a voice, a shrill squawk, "I will! I'll roll in the rushes with any boy! Let me through!"

If the young men had laughed before, now they roared, and made way for someone to come forward. And through the crowd came – an old woman. An old woman who waved her scrawny arms above her head and crowed like a cockerel as she came.

Elfgift backed away from her, shaking his head. He was ready, even eager, to hurt any of these braggarts; and he would have fought Jarnseaxa, had she been there – but to fight any other woman, untrained in anything but screeching and slapping, and one grown feeble too… The anger he felt, thwarted, began to sicken him.

The old woman came clear of the crowd, and now he could see her clearly. She came stooping, but was still taller than him; and her long, swinging arms, though thin, had strong muscles beneath the skin. Her big feet, at the end of her bandy legs, stamped firmly on the floor. Long, greasy hair hung in strings before her face, making a cage through which her glinting, squinting eyes peered. And she came eagerly.

Elfgift backed from her another step, and the on-lookers cried, "He cringes, he runs!" So he stood, and would not take one more backward step.

On came the old woman, and before her came a waft of stink like the stink from a cattle-shed. The gust of air from her mouth blew her grey hair towards him, and stank like bad meat. He turned his face aside, but thought he would stand fast against her, and take her slaps, but give her none. Her first blow rang his head like a hollow bell, and knocked him flat.

A loud cheer went up into the rafters from the onlookers. Elfgift lay bewildered on his back. A shadow fell across him, and a stink came to his nose, and it was the old hag, reaching down to take his tunic in her two fists and haul him to his feet again. The grip of her fingers tore the worn wool. No sooner were his feet under him than she let go of his tunic, pulled back her arms and let swing at him again. This time he put up his arms and blocked her blows, but still she staggered him, and his arms felt as if they had been struck with an iron bar. He saw her drawing back her arms for another cuff.

"After the third, I hit back!" he shouted.

She shrieked something, which was lost in the

noise of laughter from the watchers. It was only after her third, bruising blow had knocked him to his knees that he made sense of what she had said. "Never think lightly of an opponent!" Then he knew that if he wished to live, he must begin to fight. He scrambled to his feet while she was gathering herself for another effort, and dodged around her. She turned, faster than he had thought her able, and her long, gaunt arms shot out to grab him. He ducked under them and ran around her again, seized her by the waist from behind and hoisted her feet from the earth floor. She twisted in his grasp, and gave him blows with her elbows, but quickly seemed to weaken. He felt her sag, and dumped her on the ground. Immediately she whipped round on him and gripped him in a wrestling hold, breathing her foul breath into his face until he grew dizzy from it and feared he might faint. He knew he must settle with her quickly, before the stink withered him. He put out all his strength, and struggled with her until he felt his joints cracking – and she gave back as good – until, little by little, he felt her fail. Little by little her left knee bent, and he gritted his teeth and fought against her – and she sank until her left knee touched the ground.

There was the clangour of a knife beating on a shield, and a man shouting, "Stop! An end! An end!"

Elfgift, glad to make an end of the fight, let go of the hag and sprang back from her, warily prepared for some treachery. But the hag slowly got up from her knee and, falling back, sat heavily on a bench and mopped at her brow. Sweat flew in droplets. She breathed heavily, like a gale. But the jeering of the men gathered in the hall had fallen quiet, and Elfgift, looking about, found no sneering or smiling faces. All were looking at him solemnly.

"The hero-braids are yours by right," said the young man with the knife and shield.

"The highest seat in the hall is yours," said another.

Elfgift thought they were making a joke of him again, and looked from face to face suspiciously. His old tunic, torn and mauled by the hag, fell from him and left him naked.

The young man sheathed his knife, gave the shield back to its owner and jumped down from the bench.

"We must give you clothes," he said. "And arms. You shall make a choice from the best of our weapons."

Elfgift avoided the man's friendly touch, which would have brushed his shoulder. "All this, because I knocked an old woman about? Has it been an entertainment for you – who would have been dishonoured by fighting a slave?"

"Look at that poor old woman!" said the young man, and Elfgift looked past him to where the woman sat on the bench, her head bent down so that her hair hung to her feet, hiding her. But now the hanging hair was broadly streaked with red, as if rain had drawn rust from it, and instead of being tangled in greasy strings, it was a smooth, shining fall.

"Don't you know her?" asked the young man. "When we saw you force her to her knee! Then we knew that you had earned the hero-braids."

The seated woman raised her head, throwing back her red, grey-streaked hair. The face that smiled at Elfgift from beneath the hair was that of Jarnseaxa.

He was caught in a moment of relief and gladness, of dizzying happiness that made his head whirl like drink. He stared, and could not help grinning with pleasure. Another test: that was all. He was not abandoned.

While he still stared, people came clustering round him, bringing clothes: a fine undershirt and drawers of linen, a tunic of fine wool, dyed a clear scarlet; a belt and boots of leather.

But Elfgift took no notice of the clothes. He only stared at Jarnseaxa, who rose from her bench and came towards him. Men fell back to make way for her. She was no longer dressed like a Battle-woman, but in a long dress of scarlet wool. On her breast was displayed a golden necklace of many intricate links, and around her waist was a belt of golden plaques. She put her hand on his shoulder and kissed him. Smiling, she said, "I have made a fool of you. You should remember that even a hero can be made a fool – maybe it's even easier with a hero than with others. Do you hate me for it?"

"I love you, lady."

She smiled as if she didn't believe him. "Even now you know that I am that stinking old hag you fought just now?"

"You've given me hard knocks before, lady. And if you make yourself ugly – well, I know how beautiful you are."

She laughed, and leaned close to him, and he caught a whiff of the animal-pen stink that had hung about the old woman.

"But what if," she whispered, "that was my *true* shape, and I only make myself seem beautiful? What if I am truly ugly, and can be uglier still? Do you still say you love me?"

Her words rang true, and seemed a threat. A slight shudder ran through him. He couldn't tell if she was speaking the truth or not; but he knew she was trying to test him. So he put his arms around her, and kissed her, and said, "If that's so, lady, then it's salt to your meat. I can't eat unsalted meat."

She laughed, and pushed him gently away from

her, saying, "Now you must be armed, and not with sticks!"

The young men of the hall were bringing shirts of mail, helmets, shields and swords. Elfgift wanted to look at Jarnseaxa, and not at them, but they kept holding the things before him and calling his attention to them, until he was quick to choose among the things, simply to be rid of the chore. He chose a shirt of mail so finely made it folded like linen; and a masked helmet such as only kings and athelings wore; and a shield decorated with golden dragons.

And then they demanded that he choose a sword. Many were laid before him, their hilts bound with polished bronze wire and set with polished stones, or engraved and inlaid with silver. When they were drawn from their sheaths they had blades that shimmered with damascened patterns beaten into the iron by the smiths: snakeskin patterns, shimmers of waves, sheaves of wheat. The swords were named: Worm, Reaper, Fish-Tooth... While he was looking at them all, Jarnseaxa came to him and took his arm.

"Let me show you," she said, "the best sword ever forged."

She led him to the centre of the hall, to the living tree that held up the roof. There was the sword he had glimpsed earlier. Two lips of healing wood held it.

The hilt was plain, black, bound with wire of grey iron. It seemed the sort of sword turned out by scores, with no time wasted on making them beautiful. But if Jarnseaxa said this sword was the best... Elfgift put his hand on the hilt. "Wait," said Jarnseaxa, and rested her hand on his. "Its name," she said, "is Woden's Promise."

Elfgift withdrew his hand.

"Woden loves me," she said. "This is His gift – His promise. He oversaw its forging, and He drove it into my roof-tree – and I left it there for whoever dared to take it."

Elfgift knew that he should take the sword; that she wanted him to take it. And if it was the best sword ever forged, then he wanted it himself... But Woden was not a god it was wise to have dealings with. He gave courage and victory in battle. He also sent terror and death.

"There is no better sword than this," Jarnseaxa said. "So well made is it that its user feels no weight in his hand. So sharp is its edge that the air moans, wounded, at its passing. And the pattern beaten into its blade is the knot of the battle-fetters. It spreads fear and panic among those it is used against."

"There is more," Elfgift said. "Woden never made so simple a gift."

Jarnseaxa smiled. "The sword brings its owner victory – that is Woden's Promise. But promises are made to be broken. Whoever uses the sword must remember that, every time it's drawn, it must be blooded. If ever sheathed unused, it will turn against its owner."

Elfgift looked her in the eye. "And if that bargain's kept?"

She laughed outright. "I made a fool of you, but you have much sense. No, even if you faithfully keep that bargain with the sword, it will still turn against you, and you will never know when. Woden keeps His promises, but He always breaks them."

Elfgift nodded. The God Woden had many names, to be used by those afraid of invoking Him by naming Him too plainly. "The Treacherous God" was one. Woden's promise of victory was always, always broken, and turned to maiming or death. Those who followed the god, and asked for victory, must also accept that. Elfgift's hand fell away from the sword's black, iron-bound hilt.

Jarnseaxa watched. "So have all drawn back from it. No one wishes to grasp at their own death – so the sword remains sheathed in the tree. Take one of the other swords, they are prettier. You won't have the future you could have had, but it will be a quieter one, and longer."

Her voice was cool and she half turned away. Elfgift could not bear it. He grasped the hilt of Woden's Promise, pulled, and brought the blade's length from the wood. It came easily, the iron glistening with reddish sap.

Elfgift held the blade between his hands and studied it. From end to end of the blade, on either side of the gutter that ran down the middle, was a tightly twisted pattern of triangular knots: the sign of the battle-fetters. The workmanship it must have taken to work that pattern into the iron made the mind stagger. Wayland himself must have had the making of that sword. He tried it in the air, and the air did moan, and the sword seemed to weigh no more than his own hand.

"You've drawn it," said Jarnseaxa, "so now you must blood it." She raised her voice and called, "Atheling!"

Elfgift turned, and saw the crowds of men who had filled the hall suddenly melt and fade away, like smoke fading into the air. Through the smoke came – Elfgift started back in shock as he recognized the figure as himself. The same height and strong, slender build; the same face and long, fair hair.

"Here," said Jarnseaxa, "is a lamb for the blood-ing of your sword. His wish is to kill you, so you need feel no guilt about killing him."

Elfgift was realizing that the boy was no mirror-image, but younger than himself, and with a blind, dazed expression on his face. No hero-braids hung about his face, and his clothes and weapons glittered with gold. The boy stumbled to a halt in front of Elfgift, and his expression sharpened, then became puzzled, as if he wondered at this stranger's resemblance to himself.

Elfgift felt pity for him. It was not easy to be pushed into a fight, bewildered, and without anger. The sword in his hand might need blooding, but he didn't think he could blood it on this boy.

Jarnseaxa, at the boy's side, said, "This is the elf's drop, the bastard who murdered your brother Hunting. This is the half-thing whose head you've sworn to take."

The boy straightened, his head coming more erect. His eyes brightened with anger, more colour came into his face. Elfgift, though he took no backward step and stood his ground, felt a despairing fear – not for himself, but for the boy. This boy hadn't been trained and hardened by the Battlewoman who was urging him on to fight. If Elfgift, trained as he had been, fought this boy, it would be simple murder, a mere feeding of the terrible sword in his hand. And yet, what did that matter? Jarnseaxa, his lady, wanted him to kill the boy – that much was plain – and what was the life of one boy more, or less, in the balance of things? Trained as he was, it wouldn't even give him much trouble. And if he felt sorry for the boy now, he would soon forget that. Many times he had felt a passing regret for the small lives of sheep and pigs and ponies. It had never prevented him killing them, or eating them.

Still… He tossed the sword to his left hand and held out his right to the boy. "I killed Hunting Eadmundsson, but only after he had killed my people … and if he was your brother, then we are half-brothers, and I have no wish to kill you, brother."

At that, the anger in the boy flared. "You are no brother of mine, no brother of ours! Half-thing! Bastard! Slave!" The boy dragged his gold-hilted sword from its scabbard with an iron screech, and brandished it, but hung back, perhaps unsure of himself, perhaps still not angry enough.

Elfgift felt his own anger rise, and his own muscles tense for the fight. It was instinctive; the unthinking pounce of the cat on the running mouse or fluttering bird. He gritted his teeth, and held his anger back. He repeated, "I have no wish to kill you."

It only increased the boy's anger. He lunged at Elfgift, but, young and agile though he was, he was too slow, while Elfgift became the training he had been given and side-stepped easily, turning to meet the boy's next attack. And as the boy came, Elfgift's arm, and the sword he held, flew to deliver the death-blow. His muscles were strained as he forced himself to change the stroke and let the boy pass him unhurt. He knew that, if he kept the sword in his hand, he would kill the boy – and the anger in him rose joyously to that thought. For a moment he *wanted* to kill the boy.

He opened his hand and let Woden's Promise fall from his grip. It hit the floor with an almost musical sound. As the boy came at him again, Elfgift caught his sword-arm, twisted it up and back, and kicked the boy's feet from under him. The boy hit the floor hard and lay winded. Elfgift trod on his sword-arm, stooped and wrenched the sword from his hand, and threw it aside.

"I don't want to kill you," he said.

Jarnseaxa picked up Woden's Promise and held it out to Elfgift. "If you sheathe it unblooded, you won't live to draw it again." And she looked down at Wulfweard, sprawled on the floor.

Elfgift took Woden's Promise from her, and looked at her. She looked him in the eyes and smiled at him. His lady wanted him to kill the boy.

He looked down at Wulfweard – his enemy, and a brother of the family who had murdered his family. He tightened his grip on Woden's Promise and raised it over the fallen boy.

CHAPTER 11

The Weaving

At the Lady's call, Wulfweard started forward, and the crowd around him, that had been pressing him close, faded like ghosts. The walls of the great room about him seemed to fold and change, and yet be solid walls when he looked at them. The otherness of the Other World dizzied him.

He walked forward across a hall which he felt to be crowded, but which his eyes saw to be empty, and there, standing before him, was a tall young man, naked and long-haired, holding in his hand a dull sword. For another dizzied moment of fright or relief or hope, he took the man for one of his brothers. And then he saw it was himself. And then that it wasn't himself, for he wasn't naked, but a man more like himself than either of his brothers. The hair hanging on either side of this man's face was plaited into several fine braids, but the rest of the hair hung loose, below the shoulders. The body was thin, with the braced collar-bones, ribs and hip-bones showing clearly, but also strongly muscled. And – naked and armed with a sword – it stirred memories of old stories, of Other World warriors who rode with the Battle-women, dedicating themselves to Woden and fighting in the shapes of bears and wolves. Wulfweard shivered with the cold, superstitious fear that can seep, like cold water, even into one ready to fight.

And then the Lady said, seeming amused, "This is the elf's drop, the bastard who murdered your brother Hunting. This is the half-thing whose head you've sworn to take."

His anger rose readily, though he had feared it would not: anger at a brother's loss, anger at the thing's presumption, to dare even to speak to a member of the Twelve Hundred, let alone to kill; but when the thing spoke and called itself his brother, then he wished whole-heartedly to kill it, and dragged his sword from its scabbard. But, when the sword was raised, it seemed hard to drive it forward at that figure – though whether he was held back by a sort of love for the likeness of his brothers and himself, or by fear of a creature so like the carved ghost-warriors in the old god-house, he couldn't tell.

But he had come there to kill the thing. He couldn't go back – if it was possible for him to go back – and say that he had been afraid to attack. He would be called a coward and a word-breaker. And as the thing was naked and without a shield or helmet, armed only with a sword, it would be easy. Wulfweard struck to kill.

His blow struck nothing: the thing he fought, like the Other World creature it was, simply vanished from before his sword. He turned as quickly as he could, to find it again, and then his head whirled, and the floor was a hard blow at his back and all the breath was knocked from him in a shout. His sword-arm was pressed against the ground by the creature's bare foot, and the creature stooped, its long hair falling forward and flailing him, and tore the sword from his hand. Straightening, and throwing the sword aside, the creature said, "I don't want to kill you." It no longer held its own sword.

The creature stepped back, as if it would allow him to get up, but then the Lady came to its side, and she carried the black-hilted sword, whose dull grey, iron blade rippled with beaten patterns. "If you sheathe it unblooded," she said, "you won't live to draw it again." She looked down at Wulfweard, and he flinched at the amusement in her face and the bright, hard light in her eyes. She wanted him dead.

Wulfweard, gasping painfully for breath and unable to move, watched as the elf's drop took the sword and raised it above him. He should have kept his eyes open and faced his death with courage, and he tried. But when the light glittered on the sharp edge of the sword such a pang of fear went through him that it was as if the sword had struck already. The half-taken breath in his throat stopped. The blood rattled in his ears; his sight turned to smoke. He saw nothing.

The blow on his chest he thought was the blow of the sword entering him. He felt the wetness and warmth of blood, with its iron smell, and knew that he was killed... And yet his chest went on rising and falling, though every breath came hard. The blood went on beating in his ears and thunderously beneath his ribs. Perhaps this was death in the Other World? He moved suddenly, rolling away from the place where he'd been lying; and then he dared to open his eyes and look about.

He had to wipe blood from his face. And there was blood on the chest of his tunic, but no wound. Then he saw, lying in the rushes not so far from him, a hand. It looked so strange lying there, so complete in fingers and thumb, so ordinary and recognizable, and yet ending at the wrist.

And looking beyond it, he saw the elf-thing, on its knees and clutching at a fore-shortened arm that sent spouts of blood to soak the earthen floor and rushes, and to stain the skirt of the Lady's gown.

The Lady said, "Were your eyes closed, hero?" Wulfweard saw her smiling at him. "The elf's drop drew the sword's edge across his own arm, thinking to feed the sword on his own blood and spare you. But that sword is not so easily cheated. It bit off his hand."

Wulfweard turned his eyes to the half-thing, to its stiff and whitening face, which was almost his own, and which was dying.

Not bothering to get to his feet, Wulfweard floundered over the small space between them and seized the bastard's arm in his own hands, clapping one hand over the stump, squeezing the flesh as the blood sprayed over his face, desperately trying to stop the bleeding. But still the blood spurted out between his gripping fingers, and the bastard sagged.

The Lady stepped close to Wulfweard in her bloodied skirts, and laid her hand on his head. He felt his hair move, bristling, at her touch, and a shivering lightness seemed to run through him. She stooped low and said quietly, "All you have to do is name him with his true name." And, when Wulfweard's mouth opened, but no sound came out, she repeated, "Speak his true name. Speak truly now."

Wulfweard's tongue stammered among the possibilities. Always he had heard this man called "the bastard", "the thing", "the elf's drop" – yet somewhere in his mind was another name. "Elfgift?" he said, and shouted the name aloud again. But the bleeding didn't stop.

"His *true* name."

"I don't –" But he did know it. "Elfgift Kingsson. Elfgift Eadmundsson." The bleeding had slowed, pumping more slowly. Was it stopping, or was it only that Elfgift was closer to death? "Half-brother – brother. Elfgift Atheling."

The bleeding stopped. Elfgift cradled his wounded arm against his chest and, breathing hard, raised his head to look at Wulfweard. His face was as white as a bleached bone, and his eyes stared from it, brilliant, holding every shade of blue. His long hair fell down over his shoulders and chest, dappled now with blood.

Half-thing! Wulfweard thought and pushed himself away with his hands and feet, scrabbling through the herbs and rushes on the floor. He sat on the floor like a child and stared back into Elfgift's eyes. He was angry with himself now, for not killing the thing. He had been sent here to kill it, and it owed him its life for his brother's life. The knowledge that it had spared his life made him angrier still. He felt something like pain as he remembered admitting the thing to be his father's son and his brother.

Elfgift said, "Brother. Thank you."

Wulfweard's throat became so tight, it was as if a strong hand was choking him. Tears prickled in his eyes, and he was angry because he didn't know why – and then angry because he did know why. He had liked the word "brother". He had no wish to kill Elfgift. And yet it was a bastard and a half-thing and owed him a life.

The Lady passed close by them both, her skirts swinging to her stride and lifting the floor herbs with the draught, so that she was followed by a faint, sweet scent. She moved her hand in the air, as if she drew aside a heavy curtain, and seemed to draw aside the very air, changing everything around them with a gesture.

She had drawn the smaller hall around them, small and dark, and lit by the red fire burning in the central hearth. But for all its solidity, Wulfweard was troubled by a sense that, at the edges of his vision, and behind him, the solid walls were changing into something else – into open stretches of forest, perhaps, into lake-sides, or perhaps simply into emptiness, into the great, dark, cold emptiness that underlay everything. He turned his head quickly, as if to catch the walls changing, but he saw only black shadows bobbing and flickering about the wooden walls, jumping up into the rafters as the flames leaped and dropping down or pouncing out from the corners as the flames sank. A sweet scent of wood was breathed out by the walls in the warmth of the fire, but he was not fooled. He knew that he was in the Other World, and he caught a whiff of a stronger, darker stink underlying the smell of wood and smoke and herbs – a tang of blood.

He turned his head again, half-knowing what he would see, and there it was – the loom, with the sightless heads weighting the threads, the blood dripping from the slippery web, the grey spear thrust through them. Even as his eyes saw, the web became a weave of woollen threads weighted with holed stones. The woven picture showed a battle, where angular figures wielded axes and stones. Shadows and flame light jumped and danced across the cloth.

"You see more than most," said the Lady. "Now I know why you were chosen to be sent here." She pointed to the cloth on the loom. "There you see the future woven."

Wulfweard looked at the lines of men, with their shields and upraised swords and spears, but it was Elfgift who spoke. Still cradling the stump of his arm, he said, "The future is all of battles?"

The Lady smiled. "When has it been woven of anything else? And tell Me, of what is the past woven, if not of battles? But look closely – look into the borders and the close stitching – and you'll see harvests woven there and the moving of the herring shoals. You'll see marriages and ruts and straw-deaths and forests growing from acorns – and being cut down. And, Wulfweard, you will see woven there that Elfgift will be king of your land, because I wish to keep it for Myself and to save it."

Wulfweard looked at Elfgift, and felt again the painful struggle of liking and hatred. He made himself laugh, and said, "That thing can't be king."

The Lady said, "I will it."

"It's maimed. A king must be whole. It's in the law."

"Then he must be made whole," the Lady said. "Make him whole, Wulfweard."

As if her voice had pulled the strings of his tendons, Wulfweard got to his feet, and then stood wondering why he had. He looked at the severed hand lying in the rushes, and then at Elfgift's blanched face, so beautiful and so like his own, and he took a step towards the hand, then made himself stop. "No. My brother, Unwin, will be king."

The woman came close to him, with a quick, strong movement. The light of the fire flickered and flared over her, bringing gold from her red hair, shining on her golden necklace and belt. It lit her face from below with a red and golden light, gleaming in her eyes but casting deep shadows below them. She took his chin in a hard grip and glared at him. Her fingers hurt. No woman had ever behaved to him so, and he was shocked to stillness.

"What do you call Me?" she said.

She had never given him her name. He tried to shake his head but her fingers gripped his chin too tightly.

"When I bring warm days and flowers, when I set the fruit, when I turn the herring shoals to shore, when I fill the ewes with lambs and the cows with calves and the women with babbies – then you call Me Mother and Goddess. And when I bring ice and darkness, when I blight and freeze and kill, then you call Me Hag and Crone and Death. I – " Blood seeped between her teeth and dribbled down her chin, and Wulfweard started so violently that he broke from her grip and took a step back from her. "I am the Sow who eats Her young. I am the Wolf, who eats your young. I am the Earth who swallows you, and I – I – have given you no lordship; I have given you no dominance. I am the Sow and the Wolf and the Grain and the Earth. So I have always been, and so will I always be. And as I will, so must it be."

Wulfweard was at the centre of a storm. It crackled about him, and the fire flared high and flashed its light throughout the hall. All he saw were Her brilliant eyes, glaring with the mad ferocity of an owl's. "Your brother, and his priest and his relic – do you think that because they invent new gods, I shall cease to be? And what would you do, poor things, if I did?" She pointed to the cloth on the loom, and the shadow of her arm was thrown black across the walls. "You see battles woven there, but you know nothing of the death that will come by Unwin's way when he sets his followers, the Lords of the Earth, to clearing the forests, draining the marshes, damming the streams. His way leads to poison in every bite, and desert, and more death – oh, more death – than any battle fought by sword ever brought, more death than you can know."

But Wulfweard did know, for the flickering shadows all around him moved with the throes of death, from the struggles of a mere fly, to the flapping of a fish, to the writhing of a gnawed stag. As the flame light and shadows moved over the tapestry on the loom, the figures there seemed to twist and sink. And in every creak of the walls, in every settling of ash in the fire, every snapping of green wood, he heard the sighs, the moans, the choking of the dying.

With clenched fists the Lady said, "Lords of the Earth! *I* gave you no lordship – and if you turn from Me, I swear I shall wipe my world clean of you and begin again." Then she smiled, and the fire lost its fierce heat and brilliance, her face softened and her eyes lost their glare. "Wulfweard, sweetheart, turn back to Me. Do as I ask. Elfgift is Mine, and Me, and he shall be a king for Me. As I will, it must be."

Wulfweard went to where the hand lay in the rushes. He felt weak, and as if his body was moving without his will. He picked up the hand and took it to where Elfgift sat on the floor. Kneeling, Wulfweard took Elfgift's arm and set the hand to the stump. They both watched as the flesh reached to flesh, joining the hand and arm, and leaving a red scar. Elfgift raised the hand and flexed the fingers.

"Now," said the Lady, "he can be king."

Elfgift still sat, but he raised his head and shook back his hair. "I have one score to settle in my father's world, lady. Then I had thought to return to my mother's country. I've no wish to be a king."

She said, "You are My sword, Elfgift, and I have use for you. Did you think I taught you to fight so you could avenge the killing of a farm-wife? Every hour, thousands die, and I care not at all."

Elfgift got to his feet, a little unsteadily, and crossed the room in the firelight. Wulfweard, watching him, naked and red-lit, with his hair falling about him, thought of the old stories again.

He thought that Elfgift was going to kneel before the Lady, and perhaps kiss the hem of her gown, as one would do to a powerful saint – but instead he caught the Lady in his arms and hugged her fiercely. He said, "You are my salted meat, and for you I will be king, if you wish it."

Standing apart from them as they hugged, Wulfweard said, "Lady, if you mean the elf-born to be a king in Middle-Earth, you had best send an army with him. My uncle holds to the old gods, but he won't give his crown to my brother's killer. And my brother Unwin—"

The Lady twisted out of Elfgift's embrace and stood beside him with her arm round his waist, looking at Wulfweard.

"I share the battle-harvest with Woden," she said. "My king shall have an army. And I shall be with them, to fasten the battle-fetters on any who stand against them."

Elfgift held out his restored hand to Wulfweard. "Ride with me, brother."

Wulfweard looked away from him. His eyes fell on the loom-weaving of battles. "If the Lady allows me to go back to Middle-Earth, I must stand with my brother."

"I am your brother," Elfgift said, and still held out his hand.

Wulfweard would not look at him. "You are my half-brother. And you owe me a life."

Elfgift let his hand drop.

The Lady said, "I shall arm Elfgift, and I shall open the ways to Middle-Earth. I shan't hold you here, Wulfweard. You shall go back in Elfgift's company, riding at his side." She stooped towards him in the firelight, her hair swinging forward and then back. "Thereafter, choose sides as you will. But remember, sweetheart – no matter what god you put in your god-houses, no matter to what god you pray – *I* choose the slain."

CHAPTER 12

King Elect

With Father Fillan following close behind him, Unwin stepped through the door from his private rooms into the small hall that adjoined them, where his servants and housecarls lived and slept. At that moment, cleared of tables and bedding, it was serving as a reception room, and was crowded with a delegation of aeldermen. They filled the hall with colour, all dressed, as they were, in their finest tunics and cloaks, which had been expensively dyed yellow or red, blue or green, and further decorated with strips of embroidered braid. Every man had his long hair combed out or curled, his beard groomed and trimmed, and all were shining with gold neck-rings, arm-bands, brooches and rings, glittering belt-buckles and sword-hilts. On their most formal behaviour, they knelt when Unwin appeared, with a great noise of rustling cloaks, creaking leather, chinking metal and heavy breathing from the older men.

Unwin was quick to urge them to their feet again, smiling warmly at as many as he could. He even hurried to help up the oldest man he could see. The atheling had also taken care with his appearance. His hair, instead of being fastened back in his usual, practical style, was hanging loose about his shoulders in a waving, shifting, reddish cape. His tunic was scarlet, fringed with gold and tightly belted with a gold-studded and gold-buckled belt from which hung a seax, its hilt ornamented with garnets. A gold ring was on his every finger, and on his thumbs; a gold neck-ring at his throat, and his fur-lined purple cloak was fastened with a large, round golden brooch. Look, his appearance said silently to the aeldermen, look at what a young, virile, handsome, gracious king you've rejected. Look at these gold rings, ready to be given away as rewards for some small service. Look at the seax, ready to be used in defence of country and people. What a loss!

The oldest aelderman, whom Unwin had helped to his feet, was also the spokesman. A little out of breath, but hardly allowing it to disturb his even speech, he said loudly, for the whole hall to hear: "My lord Unwin, we have come to ask you to lead us and speak for us when we go to Athelric, to ask him to accept the crown. It is right that you should speak for us."

Another rustling and stirring ran around the hall, mixed with murmurs of agreement. Father Fillan, behind Unwin, listened closely to Unwin's answer, not so much to the words as to the voice.

Those in front of the atheling were watching his face as closely. With a young and carefree smile, Unwin said, "Gladly, I count it an honour. A better choice than my uncle couldn't have been made." There was no trace of strain or effort in Unwin's manner. Father Fillan nodded to himself, impressed. He even wondered if Unwin could be speaking the truth – though he dismissed that idea with another shake of the head.

The aeldermen drew aside and made way for Unwin as he strode between them, his cloak swinging and his long hair lifting. They all followed, with Father Fillan joining the back of the crowd. The priest was looking about him as he followed, wondering where Wulfweard was. The youngest atheling should have been there, dressed in his finest, to declare his allegiance to his uncle along with his brother. Father Fillan didn't think he could have missed the boy, even in such a crowd. But perhaps he was still at his own lodgings.

The procession made its way through the yards of the Royal Residence, watched by crowds of noble ladies, dressed in their richest best, with their children and servants around them. From further back, craning their necks, the servants and slaves of the Residence watched and cheered.

Athelric was waiting in his lodgings. A big armed chair, carved and gilded, had been set on the raised floor of the sleeping bench, and in this chair Athelric lounged casually but regally, dressed in his best gold-fringed blue tunic, and loaded with just as much gold as Unwin wore. His hair, still long and thick though fading to grey, was arranged around his shoulders to suggest that he still had plenty of strength in him; and his greying beard had been combed becomingly over his chest, to impress the onlookers with his age and wisdom. He had known that they were coming.

Unwin strode up to the chair and stood below it, very upright and still, while his cloak and hair settled about him. He paused long enough for those behind him in the hall to notice the differences between the strong young man and his elder, who was beginning to sag and fail with age. Then Unwin knelt, and those among the aeldermen who hadn't already done so, also hastened to get down on their knees.

Unwin spoke loudly. All had to hear. "Father's-brother, Athelric, it is my privilege to ask you, in the name of my countrymen, to accept the crown and be our king."

Athelric shifted in his chair, leaning forward a little. "The crown's a great weight on a man's head; a great responsibility. I think I am too far gone in years to accept it." But his hand gripped the arm of his chair as if it was the crown.

Unwin gave no sign, neither of body nor voice, that he agreed. He said, "Athelric, you are of the Royal Kin, descended from – "

Then he did hesitate. Father Fillan, at the back of the crowd, near the door of the hall, lifted his head and listened intently.

"Descended from Woden," Unwin said, loudly and firmly. "And Noah."

Father Fillan nodded to himself again. The pagans claimed descent from the god Woden. It was only polite, not to say politic, to please them by saying so. But the Christian kings claimed descent from Noah.

"You are the fittest of that Kin to rule over us. We ask you again to take the crown."

Athelric stood, and the raised floor he stood on made him tower above everyone else in the hall. Raised so, against a background of dark wood panelling, he was a fine, solid figure, the gold he wore glittering in the clear bright light from the

211

open doors. "Is it the wish of you all that I take the crown?"

The assent was given in a great cheer that rolled and boomed around the wooden walls and among the rafters.

Athelric humbly spread his arms and bowed his head. "Then I accept."

One or two cheers were called out, but were quickly stifled as the oldest aelderman held up his hand for silence. Stepping forward to stand beside Unwin, the old man called out the ritual question. "Will you submit to set your foot on the Shrieking Stone and so be tested?"

"I will submit to set my foot on the Shrieking Stone."

Now the cheering roared out again, frightening shrilling birds from among the rafters and echoing from the further walls. The servants outside in the yard set up their own cheering behind Father Fillan, and he turned to look at their excited faces, while his own became more glum. There was nothing here to make him glad. He had heard his own atheling, Unwin, claim descent from Woden, even if he had named Noah a moment later. And now here was Athelric, the next king and an unrepentant pagan, promising to be made king with all the old pagan ceremony – setting his foot in the hollow of the stone which supposedly marked the centre of the world. The stone was

212

supposed to shriek aloud when the rightful king –
that is, the fortunate king, chosen by the old gods
to bring luck to his land – set his foot on it. If any
other set his foot there, the stone would keep
silence.

The Shrieking Stone, like all other stones, was
eternally silent, but a few days after a coronation
the story always went round that the stone *had*
shrieked. And then, if the king proved to be a
disappointment, a new story began: that the stone
had been silent after all, when he stepped on it.

It was a lesson in the sin and vanity that lay in
the hearts and minds of people. Father Fillan had
told them of the True Way, of the Virgin Birth, and
the Resurrection, and still they preferred such
superstitions and lies.

The cheering had died, and Unwin's voice was
raised again. "Father's-brother! Grant me this
favour – let me be the first to swear fealty to you."
And he raised his hands, in an attitude of prayer.
Athelric, stooping, clasped his hands around
Unwin's and listened – with an admirably straight
face – as Unwin swore to be faithful to him
always, in council and in battle, in word and in
deed. The assembled aeldermen held their breath
as Athelric made the answering oath, in which he
swore to provide for Unwin and to protect him in
return for his loyal service. Then the cheering
began again, and grew louder when Athelric

grasped Unwin's wrists and drew him up on to the platform with him, and embraced and kissed him. Housecarls and servants shoved in at the door, crushing Father Fillan against a door-post, to see what was going on, and began cheering themselves. When there was such love and loyalty between the Royal Kin, surely the country was safe!

On the platform, as they came together in another manly embrace, Athelric said into Unwin's ear, "Have you heard the prophecy? Elfgift Bastard is going to return, take your head, and marry a slave-girl!"

Stepping back before Unwin could answer, Athelric spread his arms to the crowd and shouted, "Come and feast tonight in the King's Hall!" He looked to the servants at the door, who waved to him and cheered. "All will feast tonight! Food will be given out to the poor! I shall free a slave!"

The cheering began again. Unwin didn't cheer but, standing beside his uncle, he grinned and let everyone see how happy he was. Behind his smiling face he was thinking of the prophecy. He had heard it. He had already made his plans for silencing the slave-girl who was repeating it.

That night, in the hall, the white plastered walls reflected back the light of the fires, the torches and many candles and lamps until the place, long and high as it was, blazed. The light was held in the glass of jugs and bowls and drinking cups, glittered on the gold worn by the guests, and on the metal of plates. The heat from so much fire and so many people crowded together was such that faces were wet and had to be wiped on sleeves. The noise was also immense and confused: not only chattering and laughter and harp notes, but myriad tiny sounds mixing to a din of benches and chairs creaking, arms and hands bumping on tables, the clattering of dishes, the smacking of lips, the setting down of cups. And the air was thickened not only by heat but by the rich scents of roasted meat, and mead fumes, and spiced sauces. Servants, who had no right to sit, wove in and out of the tables, running to beckoning fingers, struggling past each other. At the high table, where the best dishes were served, the drink was poured by the future queen herself, Athelric's wife, Osthrida.

Unwin sat beside his uncle and smiled, and laughed, talked and drank, shouted to friends and threw bread at them, and never for an instant let it appear that anything had happened which he did not wish for. When asked why the atheling Wulfweard was not present, he pretended not to have heard the question until the questioner thought it best to pretend he had never asked it. Even when the harp began to be passed round, and man after man sang some hymn to the old gods, or some song of an old hero who swore in the name of Woden or Thunor, even then Unwin's smile and applause seemed sincere.

Father Fillan, seated at one of the lower tables, and eating the more common, everyday dishes, watched, and felt a certainty growing more heavy in him that Unwin was not pretending at all. Why, there, seated at the benches behind the high table were the priestesses of the pagan god-houses, dressed in coloured cloth and gold, like queens. Unwin had deserted Christ and returned to his ancestor, Woden, because his advantage now lay with a pagan king. The harp was making its way along the table to Unwin, and the atheling would certainly be asked to sing. If he, too, sang a pagan hymn, then Father Fillan might as well gather together his belongings and leave the country, for there would be no place or hope for a Christian priest.

The harp reached Unwin, and he took it and touched its strings into ripples of music. The whole hall hushed, and became far quieter than it had for any of the other singers. Not only Father Fillan was interested in hearing what Unwin sang. Even the servants paused, some even stood still, to hear.

" 'A boy you were when first you rode the brine-steed; young were you when first you feasted the raven. A boy in years, a man in courage, you broke the sword's sleep –' " There was a patter, a mutter of quiet applause as the listeners realized that this was no hymn or hero-tale, but an improvised song in praise of Athelric, a graceful compliment from the nephew to the uncle. " 'Old in wisdom now, though no grey-beard, the stone will shriek when it feels your foot. No grey-beard you, though old in wisdom, the stone will shout aloud at your touch –' "

Father Fillan rested his head in his hand. As the song went on, the pagan images came thicker, all battles and battle-gods, wolves and ravens and spears. There were those repeated reminders of Athelric's age, but the song announced Unwin's loyalty to his uncle – temporary as it might prove to be. In his mind, Fillan could already see his crucifix tumbling and his little church being pulled down. He asked himself if he had the courage to stay, and try to defend his church and hold his flock together. At other times, he had thought that he had. Now, with the prospect so close, his stomach shrank and his flesh moved on his bones. Martyrdom was not for him. He should return to his superiors and have them send in his place a braver man. He would have to ask per-mission from Unwin to go. No doubt it would be given.

*　　*　　*

Ebba was at table in one of the lesser halls of the Residence. She was perfectly happy, as she was warm, and filling her belly with bread and broth. Friends were around her too. Wilburga was at her side, smiling as Ebba flirted with a young man on the other side of the table. Ebba was slow to notice the two big housecarls who came and stood behind her. It wasn't until the young man opposite her fell sullenly silent and looked past her that she realized that everyone else at their table was silent too. She turned her head and looked to see what everyone else was staring at.

The men wore helmets that shadowed their eyes, and one had a shield slung at his back. Their cloaks were fastened with shining bronze brooches, and they had swords at their sides. One said, "You the Ebba that came with Thane Alnoth?"

She stared at him in fright until he repeated the question, and then she nodded.

"Come with us, then," he said.

It never occurred to Ebba to disobey, and she rose and clambered over the bench she was sitting on. She was not thinking. She was far too alarmed to think.

Wilburga said, "Why are you taking her? Who are you?"

One of the housecarls turned and gave her a long, hard stare as he assessed her standing. Having decided that she was not of much importance, he said, crushingly, "The household of the Atheling Unwin, mistress. We have orders to fetch this girl."

They began leading Ebba from the hall. Wilburga started after them. "Why?"

The housecarl looked back over his shoulder. "I don't know why, mistress. Atheling Unwin doesn't tell me all his secrets. You'd best go back to your meal, mistress."

The other housecarl had his big hand fastened hard around Ebba's skinny arm, and his grip hurt. His stride was longer than hers and, as he strode towards the door, she had to hurry and skip to keep up with him. The people seated at the tables watched them pass in silence.

They reached the door and passed from the candlelight of the hall into the sudden dark and cold of the night. Neither of the housecarls spoke as they hurried her through the Residence's yards. She was conscious of the bruising grip on her arm, and the difficulty of keeping her footing on the hard ground as she was dragged along. Apart from that, she couldn't think. She asked no questions, being afraid to hear the answers.

Her story-telling. She knew it was about her story-telling. Hadn't Wilburga warned her? Her own words came back to her: "Elfgift will come back from the Other World – he'll take vengeance on the athelings – Elfgift will come back and he'll be king…"

There rose up before them the black bulk of the Royal Hall. Yellow light shone from the windows high in its walls. A din drifted from it, of laughter and shouting, a great noise muted by the coolness and dampness of the night. The housecarls made for it, dragging her with them. As they neared the doors, the noise became louder, and there was a smell of food.

While one housecarl continued to grip her arm, the other opened the doors of the hall, releasing a great waft of heat, a scent of meat and bread, and a roar of noise. She was hustled inside, and the door was closed behind them.

There she stood, between her guards, in the Royal Hall while a feast went on around her – a feast, where only nobles were allowed. Even those people at the nearest, lowliest tables, who had turned to stare at her – even these, the least important guests, were nobles. She looked at the rushes on the floor, to hide her face. She felt filthy, ugly: a shameful object. Covering her face with her one free hand, she shook with fear and shame.

When the feast was loud with laughter, when faces were shining with sweat and mouths with grease, it was then that Athelric rose, to a fanfare of trumpets, and signalled to a long line of servants who progressed down the hall holding up large baskets of bread and cakes which were to be distributed, in the yard, and at the gates of the Residence, to whoever waited there. The people in the hall, who had been honoured with a seat at the feast, cheered their king's generosity, and raised their horns and drinking cups to drink to him.

The trumpets blew again, deafening many, but silencing the hall. Now, from the back of the hall, came two people, a man and a woman, cringing from the long stares they received, from the muttered comments and sniggers. They were slaves, dressed in the undyed woollen clothes which made a quiet note among the profusion of brilliant colours crowded at the tables. When they reached Athelric, they knelt, and received from his hands the parchments which granted them their freedom, and also gifts of new clothes – though still of hard-wearing, undyed wool – new shoes, new cloaks, and a purse of money. When the slaves stood to leave, carrying their gifts, the cheering broke out again, and someone jumped up and called on them all to drink to their king's open hand.

As the cheering died, Unwin rose from his place at Athelric's side. A quiet began to fall, and when he spoke, his voice carried clearly down the tables. "Father's-brother, may I ask a favour from you?"

Athelric turned to face him, hiding his surprise

at this unrehearsed interruption, and trying hard to hide his unease. He had no idea what Unwin was about to ask, but, as king, he couldn't afford to refuse it, whatever it was. "Ask, brother's-son. If it's within my power to grant it, I shall." That was as near as he dare come to refusing.

"I ask that you give judgement, king."

May elves strike the boy, Athelric thought: what is he at? But to give judgement was one of a king's tasks. "Judgement on what matter?"

Unwin turned and looked down the hall. Coming towards the high table were two of Unwin's housecarls and between them was a small figure, so reluctant and weak-kneed that the housecarls had to help her along with dragging hands on her elbows. She wore a baggy grey gown, and had dark hair, and a white, terrified face.

Athelric recognized her as the slave-girl who had given her account of the burning of Elfgiftsstead.

"What has the girl done?" he asked.

Leaning on the table, Unwin said, so that all the hall could hear, "This is a prophetess. She says that Elfgift bastard is the true king, Father's-brother, not you. She says that soon the bastard is going to come and kill us all, in revenge for burning his farm and killing his people. And then he will be king, and he'll marry her!" Unwin pointed to the girl, and laughed.

Athelric didn't laugh. He had to make a

judgement here, and he still wasn't sure what Unwin was driving at. He asked, "Did you say these things, girl?"

Ebba made no answer. One of the housecarls pushed her down to her knees, and she knelt, and stared at the straw and rushes on the floor in front of her, at the dried flowers, and the bones. All she could think was that she was not only in a hall full of nobles, but before the Woden's-sons themselves. They would kill her. She didn't dare listen, didn't dare understand. When Athelric spoke to her, she couldn't answer, she could hardly see the straw-strewn floor she stared at, such was her fear. They would hang her, they would take her to a bog, tie her to a hurdle and weight her until she sank – she could feel the cold water chilling her flesh as it rose about her. She hugged herself – the only comfort she had – and shivered and gulped, but could not speak a word.

Athelric repeated his question twice, but it was obvious that nothing could be got from the girl. He lifted his gaze from her and looked about the hall. "Can any bear witness that the girl has said these things?"

"I can," said the housecarl at the girl's left.

"And I," said the other.

No one else in the hall spoke. Many there knew of the prophecies the girl had made, but none were so foolish that they were going to admit it.

"And I," Unwin said. "Do you doubt my word, father's-brother?"

Athelric looked at him. "What judgement would you have me give?" It was stupid, he thought, to give any. Why make a slave-girl's words important by taking notice of them? A whipping might silence the girl in future, but no one would forget what she had already said.

Unwin smiled. "I want your judgement to be – freedom! I want you to free her too."

Athelric's mouth opened, but he bit back his repetition of the words. Instead he smiled broadly and began playing to the crowd. He embraced Unwin and kissed his forehead. "A request it gladdens me to grant! Send for clerks – let her freedom-papers be made at once. Bring her the clothes and the purse!"

Laughter and applause broke out down the length of the hall. It had been well done, Athelric admitted to himself. What the girl had said was now cancelled out. Only a man without fear and without guilt could reward the girl's accusations with freedom and gifts. The girl might go on repeating her prophecies, if she chose. No one would now believe her.

Unwin, Athelric decided, was a truly dangerous rival.

Unwin was leaning across the table to offer the girl a cup of wine and a cake filled with cream and honey. The housecarls had hauled her to her feet, but she still seemed too dazed and terrified even to take the cake, let alone understand that she had been freed. One of the housecarls took the cake from Unwin and carefully put it into her hand. She stared at it, unable to understand why she had been given it when she'd been brought here to be sentenced to death.

"To my father's-brother!" Unwin shouted. "To his crowning – to the shriek of the stone!"

And the hall around Ebba, so hot and so brilliant, burst into a great din of voices and laughter and banging on tables, startling her so much that she dropped her cake. "Now look," said the housecarl at her elbow, under the din. "All that good cream and honey wasted."

And then later, while the candles and fires still burned dazzlingly, while the heat drew the sweat from her face, while her ears rang, while her stomach squeaked at the smell of food and drink – then they brought to her a parchment and put it in her hand. And that Woden's-son she most feared – the younger one with the long, reddish hair – hung a bone plaque on a thong around her neck – hung it round her neck though she shrank away from him; and there was much noise all over again. The housecarls handed her a large pile of cloth, with a pair of leather shoes on top, and a small leather bag that rang like metal when it moved. More cheering. The cheering went on and on as the housecarls led her down the hall and out at a door into a blinding darkness and a cold so sharp that it bit. They gave her a shove and told her to go away and keep her mouth shut in future. "The atheling won't be so kind a second time."

Wilburga, wrapped in a cloak, was outside in the dark. There were some others there too – the young man she had flirted with, and people who had come merely out of curiosity. "You're safe, oh you're safe, oh thank Eostre," Wilburga said, and wrapped her in a cloak that she had been holding.

Back in their lodgings, Ebba told them, as well as she could, what had happened. She still shook, and her voice made sudden squeaks or shrilled into giggles as she remembered how terrified she had been, how certain that her death was going to be ordered. Wilburga put her arm around her and kept it there, patting her shoulder.

It was Wilburga who explained to her that the parchment was her freedom, and the bone plaque around her neck the ready proof of it.

"Freedom?"

"You're a free woman now, my love. Not a slave any longer."

Ebba was silent.

Wilburga unfolded the pile of cloth and found an undergown of good wool, an overgown, and a cloak. The little leather bag was full of money.

226

"Fetch ale!" someone said. "We need to celebrate!"

"Whatever you say about Unwin –" someone else began, and then broke off and shook her head.

Wilburga leaned close to Ebba and spoke quietly. "The best advice I can give you is to keep your mouth shut and to get away from here – as far away as you can get and as quickly as possible."

"But I can't," Ebba said.

Wilburga put her hand to the girl's cheek. "You have nowhere to go, do you, dear?"

"I could go to Alnothsstead," Ebba said. "No, it's not that. I've got to stay here. This is where Elfgift will come."

Wilburga sighed.

"Oh, Ebba," she said.

CHAPTER 13

At the Shrieking Stone

The country people walked as much as ten miles to reach the road along which the procession would ride, to see their future king and his court ride out to the Shrieking Stone. Others went to the stone itself where it lay on the hillside, and camped there, to witness the moment when a man became the Goddess-chosen king.

The ride, when it went by, was worth the walk and the wait. People who, if they owned a horse at all, owned a thick-set little pony or cob, saw troop after troop pass by of big, well-fed, fine-bred horses, groomed to shining sleekness, jingling with harness studded with silver and gold, and with glittering fringes to reins and saddle-cloths.

They could not understand how there could be such wealth in the world, to buy and feed and adorn such horses.

Among those lining the road and walking beside the procession were richer folk, who wore coloured clothes, but for the most part the crowd's clothes were the grey and brown of natural, undyed wool, years old and worn out of shape. Here and there were cloaks of leather to keep out the rain, or rustling cloaks woven out of straw. With dazzled eyes and open mouths they watched score upon score of riders pass by, every one of whom wore good clothes of scarlet, blue, bright yellow, green. Their cloaks were of bright cloth, lined inside with fur. And, in the sun, the gold they wore flashed and glared, at their shoulders, their throats, their arms, their hands. Even their belt-buckles and shoe-buckles and hat-badges flashed. How could there be so much wealth in the world?

Troops of armed men rode with the procession, and every man among them wore a shirt made of hundreds of twisted iron links, some decorated with gold studs. Every man had a shield at his back, a helmet on his head – a helmet, of iron, not a leather cap. Everyone had a spear in his hand and a sword at his side, and some carried bows and full quivers of arrows at their backs. How could there be so much wealth in the world? Still, these were warriors who would defend the borders of the country against invaders, and the ploughboys and the herders, the craftsmen and the traders who lined the road felt the safer for seeing this noisy, clanking, jangling, flashing, gleaming ride go by. They felt proud.

There was the king himself, his purple cloak trailing over his horse's haunches; and his nephew beside him, in scarlet. Both were armed, as if for battle, to show their readiness to defend their people. Both wore the masked helmets that turned them into frightening, faceless beings with faces of gold. There was so much gold and gilding about them, in their jewellery, in decorations on their battle-gear, in fringes and buckles and belts, that they almost vanished in a cloud of flashes and glitterings, of white light starred from the polished metal and stones.

Behind this glorious procession was a long, drab tail of lesser folk: servants from the Residence, country folk who had tagged on as the procession passed. They trudged along in their homespun of grey, brown and black, chattering and laughing, and sharing bread they had brought with them, and ale and water from flasks. Among them was Ebba, full of hope. Elfgift was going to come, she knew it. Before the king could be crowned, Elfgift would come to be crowned in his place. And she would be there.

230

The hill of the Shrieking Stone was one more hill in a country of hills; unremarkable except that it was known and revered as the hill of the Shrieking Stone. On its sides grew oak and ash and elm, bare of leaf now. Among them grew others: rowan, the holly showing green, the hazel and beech and elder, all left untouched on this hill because they were as sacred as the place. As the horsemen rode under the trees, the housecarls stiffened and grasped their spears. In summer, with the trees in leaf and blocking the view, this would be an excellent place for an ambush, if it weren't a sacred site, and even the shadows of the bare branches were enough to raise the hairs on the necks of the armed men. It was the more nerve-racking because here, at the foot of the hill, the whole party dismounted and, leaving the horses behind in the care of grooms, climbed the steep path leading to the top of the hill on foot. Athelric and Unwin led the way, and their housecarls, hands on sword-hilts, pressed anxiously close behind.

At the crown of the hill there were fewer trees, and at the centre of this grassy space lay a large grey stone, grown round with grass. It had not been touched with chisel, and the hollow in the shape of a human footprint which lay at the centre of the stone had not been made by any human means. It was the Goddess Herself, setting Her foot there to mark this as a sacred place, who had made the hollow – or it was one of the gods – either Woden, or Ing, or Thunor. Whichever god had made it, only a member of the Royal Kin could set his foot there safely, so it was said. Any other who did would be blasted, or withered, or would die slowly and painfully. And only at the touch of the Goddess-chosen king would the stone shriek.

The people gathered around the stone, shivering in the cold wind that blew through the bare trees, and pulling thick cloaks more closely around themselves. The poorer folk, Ebba among them, were pushed back down the slopes, even to the foot of the hill, and could only hope to hear the cheers – and the shriek – when the king set his foot on the stone. Ebba scrabbled at the steep slope, trying to climb up, but she had a hard struggle of it. Those ahead of her had no wish to be pushed out of their place. Even when, patiently, she succeeded in worming and shoving her way up the slope, she found that armed men had been posted, to keep the poorer sort from disturbing the nobles who stood around the crest of the hill.

At the top of the hill, in the cleared space around the stone, Athelric pushed back his cloak and walked forward. Those on the lower slopes could only guess what was happening from the silence that fell on the hill-top, and they, too, became quiet.

The musicians watched their moment, raising their horns to their lips. As Athelric's foot touched the hollow in the stone, they blew their horns in a deafening fanfare, more a roar than a shriek. Those closest to the din flinched, and held themselves back from covering their ears. Those on the lower slopes heard the sound and turned to each other with grinning faces, and raised their arms in the air and cheered. Only Ebba stood still, her hands to her face as she stared above the heads of everyone, seeing only the sky through the tree branches, and wondering…

Athelric, still standing on the stone, turned to acknowledge the applause and cheers, raising his arms so that his cloak fell back in graceful lines. In the bright sunlight of early spring, he fancied that he must look a fine figure – but the reaction of his people was not what he had wanted. They were staring beyond him, with shocked faces. The cheering had suddenly broken off, become silence. Some people were even beginning to point. Athelric turned sharply, and staggered a little sideways with surprise as he found that he was not alone on the stone.

Behind him, on the other side of the footprint, where the stone rose higher, stood a young man. Athelric's first glimpse was of rich cloth, of smooth green clothes, of gold braid and gold fringes: all the gold ornaments of an atheling.

Athelric took a backward step, in order to get a better look at his neighbour, and that backward step took him off the stone on to the grass. He would have stepped back on to the stone immediately if it hadn't been for the young man's face. He recognized it, and the shock froze him, as it had frozen many watchers in the crowd.

The face was his dead brother's face, Eadmund's face, but not Eadmund as he had died, an old man. This was Eadmund as he had been when young: tall and slender, strong and supple, with fair hair blazing into a white cloud around his face. Athelric tried to speak but found that he could hardly draw breath. Did Eadmund disapprove of his succession – had he come as a ghost? But why in such a shape? And ghost it must be. Nothing human could have come on to the stone behind him so. His housecarls would never have allowed it.

The people on the lower slopes of the hill, hearing the cheers suddenly cut short, looked at each other. As the silence went on, the braver ones crept up the hill's slope, trying to see past the crowd of armed men and nobles and catch a glimpse of what was going on. Ebba, hardly aware of what she was doing, flung herself against the line of armed men, trying to break through them. One took her by the arm and threw her back, and she fell, and rolled down the slope, bringing others

234

down on her. Bruised and dazed, she lay still, and saw again the sky through tree branches.

Those in the foremost ranks of the crowd stood and stared in a breath-held silence. They, watching, had seen the figure of the youth appear behind Athelric, as if he had stepped through some unseen door, or from behind an invisible curtain. Many, like Unwin, who could not remember the old king as a young man, thought that it was not Eadmund who stood there, but the Atheling Wulfweard. The men nearest Unwin had heard him speak when the boy had first appeared, though what he had said, none caught.

It was when the youth spoke that Unwin knew for certain it was not Wulfweard, and hardly knew whether he was relieved or disappointed. In a voice that carried well enough, even in the open air, to be heard by all who surrounded the crown of the hill, the youth said, "I heard horns blown, but I heard no sound from the stone."

So far was Athelric from being able to answer that he even turned to look for his nephew, Unwin, as if begging him to speak for him. But no one there, on the hillside, made any answer. There were those who would have sworn that they had heard the stone cry out at the touch of Athelric's foot, but the appearance of the youth from the air had silenced even them. And those who knew the business of the stone to be a mere show to impress the stupid were now struck with doubt, and wondered. Unwin, with a clanking of his scabbard against his mail-shirt, moved a little closer to the stone, but he had nothing to say. He only watched the face that was so like his lost brother's.

The youth set his hands on the hilts of the weapons that hung at his side: on the black hilt of a sword, and the gold-inlaid hilt of a seax. He turned his head to look about him at the armed men, at the watching ladies and nobles, and the thin braids beside his face lifted and swayed. "Who else is here of the Royal Kin?" He grinned in a wide, friendly fashion. "Let there be a fair trial, eh? Let every man of the Royal Kin set his foot on the stone, and let's see who it shouts for!"

Unwin shouted out, "My name is Eadmundsson, Atheling! Athelric and I are the only men here of the Royal Kin. Now let us hear *your* name."

The strange youth grinned again. "That can wait, brother. Why don't you come and try your chance? Set your foot in Her footprint."

Unwin, his hands on the hilts of his weapons, said, "Before you call me 'brother', tell me your name."

In his carrying voice, the youth said, "We share the same father, brother. I am also Eadmundsson, I am also Atheling."

"You are *not* Wulfweard!" Unwin cried. There were stories of the Other World beings taking on the shape of mortals, or even casting a glamour over logs of wood or bundles of straw which, for a time, they could make people believe were their friends.

The youth laughed and, behind him, from the air, from a pocket of the air, Wulfweard appeared. He was looking straight at Unwin, as if he had been standing there for a long time, invisibly, watching his brother. He was dressed, as he had left this world, in armour, but held his masked helmet under his arm, and his hair was bright in the sunlight. When they were seen so, side by side, it could be seen that, despite their strong likeness, the strange youth was the more beautiful. Beside him Wulfweard was like a golden brooch of fine workmanship, made by a clever apprentice in imitation of his master's expert original.

Wulfweard looked from his brother to his uncle and called out, "This is the successor named by our father." He jumped down from the stone and said to his uncle and to his brother, "He is to be the next king."

Now Athelric and Unwin glanced at each other. Their answer was made by the squeal of their iron blades being dragged from iron scabbards, both weapons drawn almost at the same moment. Unwin had a smile on his face.

Behind them the sound was echoed and redoubled as the men of their guards also drew their swords, ready to act as their lords ordered, even though nothing threatened them but one boy. There was sudden flurried movement as women and children hastily withdrew from the front ranks of the crowd and made for the paths leading from the hill, followed by armed men told off to protect them. Lower down the slopes there was pushing and shoving among the poorer folk as the more timid among them turned and began to bound down the rough slopes, away from the trouble, while others, eager to see whatever was to be seen and have a story to tell for the rest of their lives, climbed further up. Ebba, scrambling up from where she had fallen, saw the flurry all about her, but then climbed upwards as the crowd thinned.

Elfgift, with another wide, bright smile, made one small movement and set his foot in the hollowed footprint of the stone.

The sound pierced its hearers through. It spasmed their muscles, made hands open and drop weapons, made knees buckle, bladders loose. A grating, dragging sound, long, drawn-out, screeching, the sound of a blade on a grind-stone, or of slate dragged over slate. Ebba fell to her knees and then lay flat, her hands over her ears. She had never heard such a sound.

On the hill-top people turned wildly, looking for the source of the sound. And when they realized its source, then a still greater disorder came on them. To some, even among the house-carls, the fact that the stone had, truly, cried out with a valkyrie shriek was too much. No fear of cowardice, no thought of honour could keep them. They left their weapons where they had dropped them, and ran away. In their flight they panicked others who, seeing them run, ran too, without asking why. As the stone's shriek died away the frightened babble of the terrified rose in its place.

But to others the stone's shriek brought an ecstasy. Their hearts and minds opened to wonder: it was true! No argument was needed to convince them. Before them, on the stone, stood the Goddess-chosen king. They threw down their weapons as men who no longer needed them and clustered about the stone, to be near to this wonder, to touch the stone, and the youth who stood on it, and take strength. They laughed aloud, their faces joyful. Among them was Athelric, the throne forgotten in the joy of knowing his Goddess to be so close. And Wulfweard was at the edge of this crowd of worshippers, his body turned towards Unwin, but his face turned back towards the stone and Elfgift.

The Atheling Unwin was shaken, but he ran neither towards the stone nor from it. The stone's scream was, to him, not only frightening, but devilish, unnatural and vile. He felt the fear strike through him and responded to it with anger. This was the Devil coming to battle with the Lord to whom he had sworn allegiance, and the Devil must be fought. He looked about and saw some of his men making away down the hill, and he saw some joining the crowd of unbelievers; but there were others, mostly Christians like himself, who stood, lost, gaping. He snatched up his sword from the ground and to them shouted, "You boasted of what you would do in battle while you were drinking the ale I gave you! Will you make those words good, or will you be shamed by them?"

He saw the bewildered faces turn to him, and showed them his sword, in his hand again. "I promised you shelter and clothes, food and drink, armour and reward and I have kept my word! Now keep yours!" Some of them began to pick up their own swords, to put their shields in place on their arms. "As you swore loyalty to me," Unwin said, "so I swore loyalty to the Lord Christ, and I will die sooner than break my word!" Now his men began to rally. They cheered, and some beat their sword-blades on their shields, determined to wipe out the memory of their fear by fighting the fiercer. "Reward to the man who brings me the elf's head!" And then, as he prepared to lead them forward, he saw his brother and yelled,

"Wulfweard! Atheling! To me!"

Wulfweard, hearing, turned – and turned back again, towards the stone – but then came running to join his brother's ranks and take his place at his brother's side.

Unwin started for the stone, his company behind him, clashing their swords on their shields, raising a racket of metal and chanting. Those gathered around the stone seemed distracted, an easy prey. But as their attackers approached, the air before them shifted, and from the air stepped more wonders: armed men, shields up, swords and spears ready. The faces of these men, beneath the helmets, were the blanched, bled faces of the dead. Some were eyeless and torn, where the ravens and the wolves, Woden's creatures, had fed. Their hands, gripping the spear-shafts, were blue-tinged and blue-nailed. When they opened their mouths and raised the battle-shout there blew from them a breeze tainted with the stink of rot. Before such a sight even men in their full courage might quail, and Unwin's housecarls had already had their nerve shaken. They halted and once more fell back.

Unwin felt his own body weaken with fear, but he was the lord, the leader. He knew that if he took a step back, the rest would run. He shouted, "My Lord is the Life!" and hacked with his sword at the nearest Other World warrior. While his sword was still in the air, before it struck, he wondered, what would happen? Would the creature fly into shards of bone and lumps of carrion? Would it vanish like a dream? Before the thought was finished, he had his answer as his sword banged, with bone-jarring force, into a shield as solid as any held by his men, and backed by a force as vigorous. He got his own shield up in time.

Behind the rank of the Lady's warriors, Elfgift rallied the men who had come to him. Frantically they gathered up fallen swords, slung shields on arms, settled helmets on heads. Elfgift drew Woden's Promise from its scabbard, and felt it tremble and come alive in his hand. He had little cause to fear it today. It would be blooded well enough before it was sheathed again. It would not need to feed on him.

The two sides met in a crash of shields, a clangour of iron on iron, a clamour of full-throated yells: Woden's music. As more and more of those who had taken Elfgift's side came to the battle, so the dead warriors vanished, stepping back into the Other World from which they had come. The frail mortal men, whose flesh could be parted by iron edges, who could die, clashed again, the blow of shields shuddering through their bodies, dinning in their ears. The metal boss of a shield could smash a face, blinding, shattering the jaw and nose. The heavy swords and axes wearied the hands that gripped them. Their edges, wielded with full force, could open flesh to the bone, and break that bone, even cut through the bone. They hurled themselves into the fight in the full knowledge that they would be chopped, hacked, that their blood would pour away; that a sword-blow to hip or knee, shoulder or elbow would cripple. But they had boasted when drunk… The boasts must be made good.

It was not easy to tell whether the man you hacked at, and who hacked at you, was your friend or enemy. One man's war-gear was much like another's. The athelings were known by their masked helmets and the gold that shone about them, and their men aligned themselves with them.

Elfgift was known by his bare head, and by the speed with which he moved and twisted aside, the speed and hardness with which he struck. He needed no helmet, it seemed, because no blow could get past his shield. His sword, as he raised it, caught the light, and down its dark blade there shone a pattern of knots that, glimpsed, shrank the hearts of the men coming against him, and set panic beating in their chests. But Elfgift's men, seeing their leader fight unhelmed and laughing, seeing their opponents falter, were filled with laughter, with pride and glee in their own strength. They threw themselves forward again, and this time there was no clash of shields, for their opponents, Unwin's Christ-following housecarls, turned and ran. Nor was this a pretence, to draw their opponents out of their shield-wall to be massacred because, as they ran, they threw down their shields, dropped their spears, threw away anything that might hamper their running.

They were pursued, down the paths of the hill, down its rough slopes. They were hacked down, chopped down. So were many of those unwise enough to have stayed too close, to watch the battle. The pursuers, laughing as they killed, filled with Woden's power, were in no mood to turn their blades aside.

Elfgift, once he saw that his battle was won, did not leave the hill-top. He looked about at the bodies that lay, dead or bleeding, around the sacred stone, and he did not find it strange. The Lady shared the dead with Woden. She was a loving lady and a hard-hearted hag. You had to be glad of her smile and her love while you could. For the deaths, for the bleeding, the pain and the maiming of these men, She cared little, or She cared nothing.

He walked among the bodies, the heavy sword still in his hand. He did not want to clean and sheathe it until he was certain he would have no further use for it that day. His hand ached and trembled where he had gripped the hilt for so long. His arms shook in long tremors, from the jarring blows he had taken on shield and blade. His back ached from the effort of heaving back the weight of a man thrown on his shield. His legs trembled and ached from the strain. So he would continue to tremble for hours, just as his ears and his whole head would continue to ring and re-echo with the din of battle. He came on a man who had been gut-wounded, and looked at him a moment before putting his sword's point to the man's throat and leaning on it, as an act of kindness. Then, moving on, he came upon Wulfweard.

The boy lay half beneath a dead man who had fallen on him. At Elfgift's nod two of the men who were following him across the hill-side – following him and staring at him, fascinated – dragged the dead man aside. Elfgift crouched over his half-brother.

The boy's shield had shattered and left him undefended. His sword, still held in his hand, had a chipped and hacked blade. Blood trickled from under the calm golden face of the masked helmet. He was bleeding from wounds to the chest and arm, where his mail-shirt of heavy iron links had been sheared through like linen. Only one sword on the field could have made such wounds, but Elfgift did not remember seeing the golden mask before him in battle. He didn't remember shattering the shield or knocking down the boy's sword.

But then, he remembered little of the battle at all, except Woden's Promise hauling at his arm and exhilaration at his own quickness and strength driving him on.

Gently, Elfgift raised the head, and eased off the helmet. From beneath the calm golden mask there emerged his own face, but younger, weaker; and now marred with blood. The eyes were half-open and the lids flickered; breath sighed from the mouth. Wulfweard was still alive; but would not be for long.

Elfgift was tired, and flinched from the effort of an act of healing. He laid the heavy head on the earth again, and rose to his feet. The boy was dying. Let him die. He was so far gone that now he would slip quietly into death, without pain or knowledge of dying... And on a hill-side disfigured by so many opened and bled corpses, one more dead boy was not worthy of thought or comment.

Elfgift started away, his fascinated followers tailing after him. Wulfweard might not have been present at Elfgiftsstead, he might have taken no part in the massacre there – but he was blood-kin to those who had, and that made it fair to take his life in payment for the blood-debt. Besides – Elfgift shook his head and the hero-braids rapped against his face – the boy had left his side to fight for his brother, Unwin. So let him die in Unwin's service.

Elfgift swung round and pushed his way through those who were following close behind him. He went back to Wulfweard and dropped to his knees beside the boy. He threw Woden's Promise aside and clapped his hands roughly on Wulfweard's chest. He took a deep breath and closed his eyes, trying to calm himself and find that point of balance in his mind from where his strength would flow. Beneath his hands there was hardly any movement of breath, but there was a quick, light heart-hammering. Elfgift seemed to hear it, as well as feel it: the pulse seemed to run through his own veins. He took the rhythm of his breathing from it, and then slowed his breathing, listening to his own heart, the blood-beat in his ears. He set his teeth and bore down with his will, concentrated it like a hammer-blow: As I do will, so *must* it be! He willed the opened flesh to close and seal in the blood, he willed Wulfweard's strength to feed from his, he called the wandering spirit back with his own heart-beat. His hands glowed as they might on a cold winter's day: the heat rose into his head and made him dizzy.

Men gathered round, and saw his hair rise and crackle. They felt heat come from him, and backed away, afraid.

Elfgift knelt, with his hands on Wulfweard's chest, until he felt his strength, over-tried, sway. His head swam, and a great cold washed through him. He lifted his hands from Wulfweard and sagged sideways, catching himself on his arms before he sprawled full-length. His head hung down, and he lifted it slowly, heavily, when someone touched his arm, and looked up through a tangle of hair. Athelric was beside him, holding his helmet in the crook of his arm, and looking at Elfgift raptly, with a kind of astonishment.

Wearily, Elfgift turned from him to Wulfweard. He had not succeeded in closing the wounds, but the bleeding had stopped, and the boy's breathing was stronger. "Carry him," Elfgift said, to whoever was around – he didn't look. He hardly had the strength to speak. "Gently. Look after him."

Several men came and lifted Wulfweard up between them. Elfgift watched them move away, carrying their burden with care and fumbling steps. He still sensed Athelric at his side and, without looking at him, he said, "Count the dead."

"It is being done," Athelric said. They both knew that the strongest reason for counting the dead was to find out if Unwin was among them.

Athelric sighed, and eased himself down beside Elfgift. Worn-out, they slumped, with nothing to say, feeling the tremors running through their limbs.

Ebba had lain still on the slopes of the hill as the battle had clamoured above her, as those escaping had bounded past her. Only when the din had passed did she dare to creep up the slope to the hill's top. She was afraid, and leaped at every sound, every movement – she had no armour to guard her from sharp edges, and she was moving among men with the terror of battle still on them, ready to strike at anything that came near them. As she neared the top of the hill, wounded and dead men lay on every side. She had to step over them. Wounds and blood all around. From the smashed faces and opened muscles she quickly turned her face away, and wandered, turned from her path by the worst sights. And then, on the hill's top, she saw Elfgift, and went straight towards him, stepping over whatever was in her way.

He was sitting on the ground beside a heavier, older man; and a little fringe of armed men stood around them, staring at them. Elfgift was dressed in a mail-shirt, whose links glinted in the sunlight and, as she watched, he lifted up his head. His hair was longer than she had ever seen it, and hung in thin braids beside his face, and loose behind. The sun caught it and turned it white and gold. Every day and every night she had tried to remember the look of him; but now she saw how misty and half-formed her memory had been, and how beautiful he was. She felt love well up from the centre of her, warm, sweet and weakening: she felt her heart move towards him. She knew that he must love her because how could she feel so much, and he not feel the same?

She dared to go a little closer. On the grass close by Elfgift lay a big, black-hilted sword. Its blade was black with drying blood. She would clean it for him, she thought. Horrible as it was to her, thick with men's blood, she would take handfuls of grass and clean it – to save him the task.

She went nearer, eyeing the armed men who might chase her away. Elfgift had lowered his head again, and didn't see her. Nearer still, and she was able to crouch and reach out her hand for her sword... Just as she was about to touch it, Elfgift's head snapped up and he said, "Leave that!"

She drew sharply back, and then simply stood and stared at him, afraid that she had somehow offended him and not knowing what to say.

Elfgift, frowning, recognized her. Ebba, from his old, burned steading. He wondered how she had come there, but was too tired to think about it. But he knew the stare, the pleading, moony stare, and if he hadn't been so tired, he would have been angry. The stupid girl would come trailing after him again, abasing herself, rousing in him an irritation he didn't want to feel. And now he belonged to the Lady, who would not be kind to rivals. More than ever, there was no luck for Ebba in loving him.

He said, without anger, flatly, "Get away from here, girl. Go back to Hornsdale, where you belong."

He lifted Woden's Promise and pulled grass to clean it himself, but a man stepped forward and eagerly took it from him. Elfgift began to get up, and two or three men offered their help. He accepted the help of one; he was tired. On his feet, with a sigh, Elfgift said, "Show me somewhere I can sleep."

Athelric, getting to his feet, shouted, "An escort for the king!"

Men came running, their armour jangling. Ebba stood watching as they escorted Elfgift down the hill to where the horses had been left. Around her, around the sacred stone, men were being carried away or, if dead and from the losing side, rolled and kicked down the slopes. Elfgift didn't look back. He had forgotten her already.

She sat down on the hillside, among the dead, and sobbed. Elfgift's glass-clear eyes had looked at her so directly, recognizing her and disregarding her. His voice had been so flat, so cold. His eyes, his voice, had shown her what she was. She had come to think that she had a little prettiness, and now she knew that she was gawky and plain. She had thought highly of her two gold rings and her purse of atheling's gold: now she knew that it would not buy Elfgift's sword, or his helmet, and was hardly enough to get a poor farmer to give her a second glance. She was brought hard up against her own foolishness, and her loneliness – lacking, as she did, parents, sisters, brothers, master, lover.

A raven, huge and black, dropped heavily to the ground beside her, and pecked at the earth which Wulfweard's blood had soaked.

CHAPTER 14

Web in the Weaving

The tall, leafless trees stood black against a band of glowing red. Above the red, the sky was a deep blue, deep almost to blackness. Unwin, looking back in the direction they had come, back towards the setting sun, said, "Is my brother dead?"

"My lord," said the tired man on the horse beside him, "how can we tell?"

Unwin had seen Wulfweard fall, cut down by the elf's drop, by the black sword. There had been nothing he could do. His men had been broken and running. If he had stayed, he would have died too, and then there would have been no one to take blood-payment for Wulfweard or Hunting.

Unwin turned in his saddle and kicked up his horse, rejoining his little troop. They had run, and had reached the horses, had taken mounts for themselves and scattered the others, to delay pursuit. They rode on, in the last of the light, towards the North. To the North, if they could reach them, were the lands of the Northern foreigners, the North Welsh. They were Christian – Father Fillan had come from there – and would welcome a Christian atheling.

In the North Unwin could wait in safety for the news that would tell him if he was the only surviving atheling or not. In the North he could raise an army for revenge.

In the barracks of the Royal Residence the exhausted warriors slept; but in other halls there was celebration and excited talk, which crackled from lodging to lodging, drawing people together. A new king – Goddess-chosen, elf-born! The future could only be good.

Wulfweard lay in his own bed, in his private lodgings inside the Residence. He had been stripped, and his wounds washed and covered. Beside his bed sat priestesses of Ing and Woden, who had cut the necessary runes on slips of wood and put them beneath the pillow and bed-coverings. They sang spells as they kept watch, but both had heard that ragged clotted breathing before. One slipped a hand into the bed, and, catching her companion's eye, shook her head as she felt how cold the atheling's fingers were. Soon, she thought, they would have to change their song from a spell of healing to the hymn which guided the escaping soul on its way to the Other World.

The new king, the elf-born, had come to see his half-brother, and had laid hands on him again and tried once more to help him – but had been so wearied himself that his knees had given way. He had kept Wulfweard from dying on the battlefield but could not, he said, do any more. So the priestesses sang on, through the candle-lit night. Let the dawn come, they prayed, as they sang. So often, with a new day, came new strength, even to the dying. But, if death must come first, then so be it. It was the Goddess's part to choose the slain.

In a dark corner of the Residence, beside a store-room, Ebba lay in the dirt and wept her strength away. Then, calmer, she would sit up, wipe her face, dirtying it, and swear in a fierce whisper that she would never weep a tear more, or ever care for Elfgift or any other ever again. And then she would fall into tears once more. And often, choking with tears, she shouted out that she would hurt him as he had hurt her – and then take the words back. But the wish always returned.

*   *   *

Elfgift lay in the private apartments of the king, in the carved and gilded bed in which his father had died, and he lay in the arms of the Lady, the Hag, the Lover and the Maiden and the Battle-woman. Into his half-sleeping ear She whispered Her plans for the future. "Unwin..." She whispered, and, "Athelric..."

Stirring, Elfgift asked, "Wulfweard?"

"Ah," She said, and laughed, and whispered, "*I* choose the slain."

Have you read?

THE STERKARM HANDSHAKE

From out of the surrounding hills came a ringing silence that was only deepened by the plodding of the pack-ponies' hooves on the turf and the flirting of their tails against their sides. Above the sky was a clear pale blue, but the breeze was strong.

There were four members of the Geological Survey Team: Malc, Tim, Dave and Caro. They'd left the 21st that morning at eight, coming through the Tube to the 16th, where the plan was to spend four days. None of them had ever been so far from home before, and they often looked back at the Tube. It was their only way back.

It was when they lost sight of the Tube among the folds of the hills, that trouble arrived.

Three horses, with riders, picked their way down the hillsides towards them. The horses were all black and thick-set and shaggy, with manes and tails hanging almost to the ground. The riders' helmets had been blackened with soot and grease, to keep them from rust, or covered with sheepskin so they looked like hats. Their other clothes were all buffs and browns, blending into the buffs, browns and greens all around them. Their long leather riding boots rose over the knee. On they came with a clumping of hooves and a jangling of harness, carrying eight-foot-long lances with ease.

"It's all right," Malc said. "Don't worry. They're just coming to check us out."

"There's others," Caro said. There were men on

foot, about eight of them, running down behind the riders.

The riders reached them first, and circled them, making the geologists crowd closer together, while still clinging to the halters of the pack-ponies. The riders' lances remained in the upright, carrying position, but this wasn't reassuring.

Up came the men on foot, and the riders reined in to let them through. The footmen were all bearded and long-haired, and had long knives and clubs in their hands. A couple had pikes. Without any preamble, they laid hands on the ponies' halters and tugged them out of the geologists' hands.

"Don't argue," Malc said. "Dave, let it go. Let them have whatever they want."

Two of the riders dismounted, handing their reins to the third – a boy of about fourteen – who remained on his horse. They had a look of each other, the riders, like brothers. The first to dismount, his lance still in his hand, was probably the eldest. He was bearded, but no older than about twenty. He went straight up to Malc and began to pull the back-pack from his shoulders.

"I thought they'd agreed not to rob us any more," Caro said, taking off her own back-pack as the other dismounted rider came towards her.

"Just don't annoy them," Malc said.

As Dave and Tim shrugged out of their backpacks, one of the bearded footmen called out something – in a speech that sounded like coughing and snarling. His companions all laughed.

The geologists looked anxiously at each other. They didn't understand the joke, and were afraid of how far it might be taken.

The second dismounted rider suddenly caught Tim's hand and pulled his arm out straight. For a moment Tim looked into an almost beardless and strikingly pretty face – and then the young man was dragging at his wrist-watch, pulling the expandable bracelet off over his hand. He stared Tim in the face for a moment, and then snatched off the geologist's spectacles before moving on to Dave and grabbing at his hands too. Dave took his wrist-watch off and gave it to him.

Malc and Caro, catching on, quickly took off their wrist-watches and handed them over.

The first rider – the bearded one handling an eight-foot lance as if it were a pencil – seemed not to like the pretty one having all the watches, and a coughing, snarling argument started between them. While it went on, Malc caught sight of Caro's face, set in a grimace of fright. The other two looked much the same, and he supposed that his own face also reflected his painful uncertainty and fear.

The argument ended with the pretty thief handing two of the wrist-watches to the one with the lance – who immediately turned to Malc, grabbed his waterproof and pulled at it, snarling something.

Malc pulled his waterproof off over his head. The others hurried to do the same.

The pretty rider gestured at their other clothes. Take them all off, he seemed to mean. Certainly, when they hesitated, there were more peremptory gestures and snarled words.

Caro saw the way the footmen gathered closer as she pulled off her jumper, and she stopped, only to be shoved, and staggered on her feet, by the horseman with the lance. When she still hesitated, he grabbed at her shirt, pulling the buttons undone and exposing her bra.

"Caro, do as they want," Tim said. "It'll be all right. We're here."

Malc, Tim and Dave all edged closer to her, trying to shield her, but she knew perfectly well that there was nothing they could do to protect her, outnumbered and unarmed as they were. She took off her shirt, shaking with fear. There was nothing remotely exhilarating about the feeling. She felt sick and desperate, and wished she'd never left the humdrum safety of the 21st-side.

They took off all their upper clothing, but still weren't undressing quickly enough for the liking of their attackers, who dragged at their arms, and pushed them, to hurry them up. One of the footmen, by pointing, made it clear that he wanted their boots – and then, when they were seen to be wearing thick socks, the socks were pulled off their feet, and their trousers tugged at.

They stripped down to their underpants, which caused hilarity, and the pointing and jeering was as threatening as the shoves.

Despite being so funny, their underpants were taken too, leaving the Survey Team standing naked in the breeze. Their skin roughened with goose-pimples.

Their attackers walked round them, examining them from all sides, pointing, making remarks and laughing. Caro closed her eyes and held her breath, feeling her heart thumping heavily under her breastbone.

But then the riders mounted again, and the whole party left with their loot, the footmen leading the pack-ponies.

The Survey Team were left, shaking but still alive, to walk over rough country, naked and bare-foot, all the way back to the Tube and the 21st.